Endless

JACLYN WEIST

Endless

JACLYN WEIST

Copyright © 2014 by Jaclyn Weist

Second Edition © 2018 by Jaclyn Weist

Cover © 2017 by Rachelle Hardy
Print Edition ISBN: 978-1-944137-22-9

Dedication

For my dad—I'll always be your little girl.

Acknowledgments

Have you ever had a recurring dream? I've had a few over the years. In one dream, I would walk into a hallway and find stairs that had no end. I'd start climbing them and could never find what I was searching for. As time went on, I'd try to avoid the stairs, but I would still get lost.

Fast forward several years, and I was looking for a fun idea for a book. This dream came to mind, but I had no idea where I'd go with it. When I first started writing, it was dark. Darker than I'd ever written before. Things were crazy with family, trying to sell a house, and health issues. As I wrote, I'd bounce ideas off my friend, Jenna Eatough, and we'd come up with the next plot point.

But then things got better. Life smoothed out, and I was happy again. The Gothic feel to my book didn't work anymore. And then brilliance struck. I knew what I wanted to do. I took most of the elements Jenna and I had gone through and went a completely different direction.

Thank you, Jenna, for helping me with the ideas for this book. Thanks for your friendship and thanks for taking me for cupcakes when I needed to get out of the house.

Thanks to my mom for reading my book and for

loving it so much. I'm going to frame the note I got from you when you finished it. It meant the world to me.

I struggled to find the perfect cover for my book because I wanted something that perfectly defined what it was about. A few pictures came close, but then I decided I wanted to do it myself. Although, when I say myself, I really mean with the help of the best family I could possibly ask for. Kristen made the nightgown; Rachelle offered to take the pictures and make the cover; my niece, Katy, was happy to be the model; and Charlotte let me make her day just a little crazier while we did the shoot. It's been fun to see my dream come to life.

I wanted to do things a little differently with my characters this time. I chose my family members as Sydney's friends, and it was so much fun to see how they interacted. The dialogue and actions were so easy because I knew who they were. So thank you, Jill, Ben, Charlotte, and Eric for letting me borrow your children. I hope I did them justice.

Thank you to Adam Olsen for helping me find a few spooky places to do photo shoots. Thank you, Beth Moore, Aften Szymanski, Kim Searle, Jenna Eatough, and Tamera Westhoff for beta reading my book. You had great feedback that made the book pop.

I wouldn't be able to write without the help from friends. I want to thank those on iWrite chat and Sprint Writers Central for being such amazing cheerleaders.

And for staying up until late while I finished the last few chapters of the book.

Thank you to my little family for your patience and your ideas for my books. Thanks for letting me borrow a few of you for this story as well. I'll get the rest of you soon. Thanks, Steve, for putting up with the moments when I'm too far into my book to recognize that anyone is talking to me. I love you lots.

And most of all, thank you to my readers for enjoying my books. This year has been a wild ride, and I couldn't have done it without you.

Chapter One

Someone was here. I had been running all night, and I was exhausted. I kept looking behind me as I climbed the stairs, but I couldn't see anything. My heart raced and my breathing grew heavy. I needed to get off these stairs, but I couldn't find the exit. I could never find the exit.

I heard something up ahead and stopped, blood draining from my face. I whipped around and ran back down the stairs as fast as I could. I slid a couple of steps, but no way was I stopping.

The stairs had been plaguing me for years. Every night, I would dream of them—never-ending steps that took me nowhere. Some nights, I'd wake up sweating because someone followed me. Someone who didn't belong.

I don't know what triggered the dreams. I just knew that even when I was awake, I could see that staircase.

"Sydney, are you paying attention?" a nasally voice asked.

I jumped, waking from the stairs and back into my English class to find everyone staring at me. "Yes. Sorry. What were you saying?"

Mr. Stanger glared at me. "I take that as a no. I need your test. I assume you're done?"

I looked down at the blank page and my stomach dropped. "Um, no. Could I have just a couple more minutes?"

A few of the students snickered. Great. Another reason for them to laugh at me. I ignored them and kept my eyes on Mr. Stanger, pleading for a little mercy.

He grumbled. "Class dismissed. Don't forget to read over the summer. Yes, school may be out, but that doesn't give you an excuse to allow your brains to forget everything. Next year is your senior year. You'll need all the help you can get. Sydney, come see me."

I used to be the teacher's favorite, but somewhere along the way, I forgot to care, and he didn't like that. I picked up my blank paper and trudged up to the front of the class.

"Look, I'm sorry I didn't finish the test. I didn't sleep well last night." Or any other night, for that matter.

He sighed. "How much did you get done?"

I glanced at the paper in my hand. The dirt in my nails distracted me. They would need to be cleaned before I got home. Julie would be angry if she saw anything that could embarrass her. Never mind that she was the reason for the dirt in the first place.

"Sydney? How much?" Mr. Stanger urged.

I handed him the paper, figuring it would answer the question for me. My heart thumped in my throat. Dreams of college were long gone after Julie spent everything Dad had saved up for me, but I'd hoped for scholarships. It didn't look like that would happen either.

"This is blank. You didn't do anything?" The disappointment was evident on his face.

"No. I must have dozed off." I clenched my fist, willing the tears to remain unshed.

"You fell asleep." He sighed. "Sydney, if I give you another chance after school, would you at least *try* to take the test?"

I felt something I hadn't felt for a long time. Hope. "You'll give me another chance?"

"You have a D in the class, and yet you answer every question I throw at you correctly. Yes, I'll give you another chance. No telling anyone, though. I don't want to lose my reputation." He turned to his desk and scribbled a note. "Get to your next class. And Sydney? How about you stay awake?"

"Thank you, Mr. Stanger." I smiled, relieved. Not many others had given me this kind of break.

I did my best to pay attention for the rest of school. The other kids made it rather difficult as they snickered and made faces at me—always when the teacher wasn't looking. The bags under my eyes, falling asleep in class, staring blankly ahead, avoiding friends I used to hang with—none of those things had gone unnoticed. I'd heard the rumors flying around about why I'd stopped caring. Nothing came close to the truth.

There was no way they could know what was happening at home, or what plagued my dreams.

When the final bell rang, everyone cheered and ran for the doors. Summer vacation had started. I made my way back to English, where Mr. Stanger waited for me. He silently handed me the test.

I sat down and stared at it for a minute before flying through the answers. It covered subjects from the entire year—Mr. Stanger was known for being tough—and I remembered most of it from the times I had actually studied. It helped that English was my favorite subject.

I handed him the paper and grabbed my bag.

"Why don't you wait a moment while I grade your test?"

"Oh, right." I sat down in a desk and pulled out a book to read while I waited. The clock ticked loudly, distracting me from the words on the page.

"Sydney? Here you go." He held out the test. "Good luck with everything. You have a lot of promise, if you'll apply yourself next year."

I looked at him in surprise. "Really?"

"You just answered every question correctly. I could accuse you of cheating, but no one else is here to give you the answers. You know your stuff. Well done." He smiled.

"Th—thanks. I appreciate that, Mr. Stanger." I smiled back and left the classroom feeling a little lighter than when I walked in.

"I'm home!" I called. *Not that anyone cares.* Kaylee and Sarah must have gone shopping. Good riddance. I could catch up on housework before they gave me more. Never mind that this had been *my* house for as long as I could remember.

I threw my backpack on my neatly made bed. The fact that the blanket was tattered and faded meant nothing. It was one of the only things I had left from my mom. I changed out of my school-enforced sweater vest and plaid skirt and into a pair of old sweats and a T-shirt.

I glanced outside and saw Dad's sleek black BMW pull up in front. This day just got better and better—something that rarely happened for me. I squealed and ran for the front door. He had been gone on business for three weeks, and I had missed him terribly. He was the only one who understood me.

Dad opened the door, and I threw my arms around his neck. "Daddy! You're back!" I had never stopped calling him "Daddy," maybe because he had never stopped calling me his "little princess." Being the only two people in the house for ten years would do that.

He dropped his briefcase and squeezed me back. "Hey, honey. Did you really miss me that much?" He let go and searched my face. "You're still not sleeping?"

I knew I couldn't fool him. "No. And I'm exhausted. I fell asleep in class today."

"The stairs again?" He frowned.

"Yes. And it's getting worse. Did you figure anything out?" One of the reasons Dad traveled was to find a cause for my dreams. Not that he told my stepmom that—she figured a good cure for my "hallucinations" was taking me to a shrink. When that didn't help, she didn't want to deal with it and decided to send me off to camp. If she knew what he was really doing … who knows what she would have done.

He sighed. "No. I didn't. I thought I'd found a charm you could wear, but when I caught the guy selling the same charm to transform someone into a cat, I didn't think you'd want to try it. Oh, but I did bring you this." He pulled out a bar of Swiss chocolate. My favorite.

I took it from him and hugged him again. "Thank you! And thanks for not getting the charm. I don't feel like being a cat. Although, maybe cats don't dream." I picked up his briefcase. "Come on. I'll get dinner started, and you can tell me about the important banker stuff you did." The chocolate would wait until I was alone so I could savor every bite.

"You don't need to cook, princess. Let me take you all out for dinner." He picked up his other bags off the porch and followed me in the house and back to the kitchen, where he dropped them by the counter. I'd get them later. He was the one person I didn't mind cleaning up after.

"You've been out to eat every night since you left. I'll make you spaghetti and meatballs. Your favorite." It would also be nice to cook for someone who actually appreciated it.

"Your mom's recipe?" he asked hopefully. His eyes softened, and he played with a napkin that sat in front of him.

"Of course. Is there any other?" I smiled and pulled out the pots I would need. Mom had been a trained chef and used her best recipes on us. Even though I was only four when she passed away, she had taught me her love of cooking. I had found this recipe a few years back in one of Mom's cookbooks, and it always brought a smile to my dad's face.

"Has Julie treated you well?" He started shredding the napkin. "And where did she go?"

I shrugged. "About the same. And I don't know. I haven't seen her or the girls since I got home from school." I couldn't help my bitter tone. I chopped the garlic a little harder than I normally would and slid it into the pan.

"She loves you. You know that, right?" By that time, the napkin was a pile of scraps.

I raised my eyebrows. "You've got to be kidding me. Is that why she's sending me away?" I chopped the onions and slipped those in.

He smiled. "I think it will do you some good. Maybe you can even make a friend. Or—dare I say it—a boyfriend." He wiggled his eyebrows at me.

"Yeah, like that'll happen. A friend would be nice, though." I dumped in the sauce and mixed it up before getting water ready for the noodles. The rich aroma of the garlic filled the air.

"Amy still isn't talking to you?" he asked. He pulled out his phone and typed in a quick message before putting it back in his pocket.

I shook my head. "No. She's too busy with Evan." Not that I minded—I'd heard the rumors she'd spread about me. I was done with friends who stabbed me in the back.

"How about you and I go to the batting cages

tomorrow morning? I haven't played for a long time, and my company is supposed to be starting up a team for the city league." Dad came over and dumped the noodles in the water and took a spoonful of sauce. "Mmm, just like I remember it."

I grinned. "Thanks. I try. And seriously, it would be awesome if we could go tomorrow." I adjusted the heat on the sauce.

"I'm going to change out of this suit. I'll be back to set the table in a minute." He left the room, and I couldn't help but smile. I would have my dad to myself for the day.

The kitchen door leading to the garage crashed open. Julie came storming in, arms loaded down with bags. "Sydney, why didn't you call and tell me your father was back?" Her pencil-thin eyebrows came together in an angry scowl. I could almost swear there was smoke coming out of her ears.

"I'm sorry. I wanted to have di—"

"That's no excuse. You know how much I looked forward to having him home. Now take these bags to Kaylee and Sarah's rooms." She dropped all but three on the ground and went into the master bedroom.

Her shriek of fake excitement and gushing over Dad echoed down the hall. I rolled my eyes and hoped Dad would see past her overdone makeup and realize what she really was.

"Oh, look. It's Sydney cooking over a hot stove again." Sarah came in and dropped two more bags with the rest. "Take those. I'm too tired." She flounced off to her room and slammed the door. Music blasted through the house seconds later. Kaylee followed behind, brushing her purse up against a vase on the table just inside the door. The vase dropped to the floor and shattered. It had been one of my mother's. Julie hated having it out, but Dad insisted. My mouth hung open as I tried to register what just happened. The sizzle of water spattering out of the pot brought me back to my senses.

"Oh, oops. Clean that up, would you? I can be so careless sometimes." Kaylee's laugh grated on my nerves as I pulled the noodles off the stove and strained them.

I grabbed the broom and dustpan and swept up the remains of the vase. As soon as Kaylee left the kitchen, I slipped the pieces into an old box so I could try to salvage it later.

I had just finished mixing the sauce and noodles together when shouting erupted from Dad and Julie's room. I set the food on the table and grabbed the dishes, wondering what was going on, but knew that Julie would flip if she found out I was listening.

"—dare you take her out instead of spending time with me?" Julie's voice echoed through the house as she followed Dad into the kitchen.

It looked as though he had aged ten years since he'd

come home. "Her birthday is coming up. I need to leave again next week, and I want to spend time with her."

"But what about me? Don't I count? Don't you love me?" she simpered.

My stomach tied in knots. I knew that trip to the batting cages was too good to be true. Julie would get her way—again. I dished up the spaghetti, clamping my mouth shut, determined not to let her get to me.

"Sweetheart, we've been over this. Please go get the girls." Dad sat down and rubbed his temples.

Julie huffed and left the room, glaring at me as she went past. Oh, I'd be paying when Dad went on his next trip.

"If you need to go with her, you can," I mumbled, handing him his plate.

"No. You need me more." He smiled and waited for the others to come to the table before he started eating.

Dinner was silent, and I was grateful when it was time to start the dishes. I went through the motions, just wanting to hide in my room before Julie could get her claws into me. I'd already forgotten to take the bags, and the girls were furious when Dad told them to do it themselves. Camp could not come soon enough.

Chapter Two

That night, the dream changed. The stairs were there, as always, but this time, instead of the evil feeling of being watched, I could see something above me that filled me with warmth. I picked up my skirts and started climbing as fast as I could.

I awoke with a jolt. My skirts? I'd been wearing a blue ball gown. Normally I wore my long white vintage-style nightgown. A glance at the clock told me that only a couple of hours had passed. I switched on my lamp, pulled my notebook out of my drawer, and wrote out the changes in the dream. I needed to find any kind of pattern so I could try to break it.

Once the notebook was put away, I flopped back on my pillow. I didn't want to dream again, but my exhaustion was overpowering. Maybe Dad should have bought me that charm. The side effects were worth it if it meant I could sleep.

I was back in the dream, but this time, the setting was a Renaissance fair—or at least, it looked like it. The gown was the same as I'd been wearing in the last dream. I sighed in relief. I could do this, right? There was nothing scary here.

Wandering through the fair, I watched in delight as jugglers went past on stilts and knights jousted on horses. I could stay here. I came to a tent and meant to keep walking, but the need to stop was overwhelming. I tried to shake it, but I found myself lifting the flap to see who was inside.

"Welcome, Sydney." A wrinkled old woman sat a table with a crystal ball in front of her. The tent smelled of incense, making me sneeze.

My stomach dropped in fear. "How do you know me?"

She laughed. "This is your dream. Come, sit. Let me tell your fortune."

I shook my head. "I have no fortune. Julie will make sure of that."

"Sit, sit, sit. We all have a fortune." She moved her hand over her crystal ball and peered into it, then gasped and looked up at me

with wide eyes. "Someone watches you. Someone dark. You must rid yourself of him. Avoid the stairs at all costs, or the one you love the most will be lost."

I jerked awake and lay there, trying to slow my breathing. My heart beat rapidly and sweat poured down my face, mingled with tears. What did she mean? I'd already lost my mom. The only other person I cared for that much was my dad. And if anything happened to him . . . I let out a sob. Why couldn't I just dream of butterflies and rainbows like everyone else?

Deciding that four hours of sleep was plenty for a growing sixteen-year-old, I yawned and pulled out my beat-up duffel bag. Packing for camp wasn't hard when I only had a few pairs of pants and a couple of shirts. Raiding Kaylee and Sarah's closets was not an option, or they'd make my life even more miserable. Besides, I wouldn't be caught dead in the frilly pink clothes they insisted on wearing. I would just have to hope that the camp had some kind of laundry place so I'd have something to wear.

Packing only took a few minutes, so I decided to read a book. I kept drifting to sleep, but I would immediately wake up every time the scene of the fair popped into my dreams. When the sky had just started lightening, I changed out of my pajamas and grabbed my baseball cap before heading toward the door. Dad always liked to be the first one to the batting cages.

The knob wouldn't budge—it was locked. I tried again, just to be sure, and then pounded on the door. "Hey! Let me out of here. Dad? Julie? I can't get out." I peeked through the old-fashioned keyhole and could see Sarah asleep on the floor in the hallway, snoring. Of course. Julie wouldn't want me going with Dad, and she apparently wasn't taking any chances. I'd escaped too many times before. "Sarah. *Hey, Sarah.*"

Sarah snorted and looked around before going back to sleep. I wondered if Julie realized she'd put the heaviest sleeper in charge of keeping me prisoner. And what was the point? I could just go out the window.

I pulled the window open slowly, making sure there would be no creaking sounds. I dropped my mitt onto the ground and climbed out, then dropped into the bushes. I made sure Julie wasn't around before running toward my dad's car, praying it wasn't locked. There was another way to get in if it was, but I didn't want to use that trick.

This wasn't the first time I'd had to escape my room. Whenever Julie thought Dad was going to spend more time with me than with her, she'd find ways to keep me from going. Telling him I was sick, breaking something I'd need to clean up, and the list went on. Somehow Dad never caught on. She must have some power over him, but I could never prove it. Thankfully, I had one thing she didn't know about.

I glanced into the car and cringed when I saw that the lock was down. I braced myself and twitched my hand to the right, watching the lock pop up just before dropping to the ground in agony.

Using magic was not the fun, exciting thing the fairy tales said it was. It hurt. It made me feel like every bone in my body was ready to break. Dad promised it would get better. You could barely tell he felt pain when he used magic now.

Once I could stand, I opened the door and slid into the backseat to curl up in a ball and try to sleep so I could regain my strength before Dad came outside.

"What are you doing here?" Julie shrieked from outside the car.

I jumped and wiped the drool off my face. Way to be smooth. "I'm waiting for Dad to take me to the batting cages."

"How did you—" She stopped and smiled at Dad, who had just come out of the house. "Hello, sweetie. I thought we were going shopping." She kissed him soundly, and I tried not to gag.

"You know I planned to go with Sydney. Why don't you go buy something to wear for tonight? I'll take you girls out to dinner." He put his arms around Julie, and I looked away.

"Okay, dear. But it better be nice." The look she gave me could have frozen hot lava. She sauntered back in the house.

I sighed. What kind of spell did that woman have on my dad? I hopped up into the front and buckled my seatbelt.

Dad climbed in. "Ready to go?"

"Yep." I felt lighter than I had in weeks.

Dad started the car and headed toward the batting cages. "So, did you sleep in the car all night?"

I shook my head and looked out the window. "I had to escape my room."

"What do you mean?" He stopped at a red light and looked over, brows furrowed.

"They locked me in. Again. Dad, they hate me." I could feel the ball of frustration growing in my stomach. I'd tried to convince him of this several times.

"They don't hate you, although I *am* going to talk to her about locking the doors. You're sure it wasn't just stuck?"

I raised an eyebrow. "She had Sarah on guard duty."

"Probably not the best choice for a lookout." He smiled and turned into the parking lot.

"*Dad.* Focus. They're trying to keep me prisoner. Can't . . . can't you just take me with you?"

"I would love to, sweetie. But the places I go just aren't safe for you."

"Dude, you're a banker. How dangerous can they be?" I climbed out of the car and grabbed my bat from the backseat. "It's summer vacation. I don't even have school to worry about."

He put his arm around me. "You know I don't travel just for banking. I have to catch those mercenaries. Besides, you're not trained yet."

I stopped walking and looked at him. "Yes, but *when* am I going to train? I can't do it at home."

Dad grinned. "I might have had a little influence on where you're going for camp."

"You mean . . .?" My heart rose in my throat.

"Yep. You're going to a magic camp."

I jumped up and down and squealed. "Thank you, Daddy!"

"You'll have to work hard to catch up. Some of these kids have gone a few times already."

"I will."

We went inside, and Dad paid for us before we went to the cages. We set the machine up for me and Dad stood outside, watching. The balls began to come at me and I got lost in the movement. I had been cut from the baseball team when my grades slipped. Getting back into the groove of smacking the ball as hard as I could helped wash away my stress. Pretending the ball was my stepmother's face helped even more.

My turn ended and I left the cage, breathing hard. I knew I'd be feeling it the next day, but I didn't care. "Your turn, Dad."

"You did really well, sweetie. You're a shoo-in for the team next year." He ruffled my hair and walked past, handing me his jacket.

"I have to keep my grades up. I don't see that happening any time soon." I sighed and leaned against the net.

Dad's phone rang in his jacket pocket. I pulled it out, but didn't recognize the number. I glanced down to see a text message.

Got it. Meet me in the usual place next week.

It was so vague, it could mean anything, but in Dad's undercover wizard job, they were usually pretty careful with what information they passed on. "Dad? You have a text."

"I'll get it in a minute. I'm almost done." He hit the last two balls and stretched his arms as he left the batting cage. "I didn't hit as many as you did, but I think I scored pretty well."

I handed him his phone. "How does it feel to get beaten by your daughter?" I grinned. Sweat dripped down Dad's face in the hot morning sun. It was definitely time to be done for the day.

"That just means I taught you well." He winked and checked the message, and his face lit up. "They have it. They found your cure."

I thought my heart would beat out of my chest. I could be free of these awful dreams! "They did? Are they sure? Because I don't want to end up glowing in the dark or something." But a cure! I could sleep again.

"I'll have to check it out when I get there. I won't buy it if the side effects are outrageous. Ready to go home? I need to call him back and work out the details."

"Only if we can get a milkshake on the way." I fluttered my eyelashes and laughed.

"It wouldn't be a trip to the cages without one." He put his arm around me, and we walked out to the car. "The big question is, what flavor do you want?"

"Rocky road. Is there any other kind?" I threw the bats in the backseat, climbed in the front, and waited for Dad to get in.

"Not that I know of." Dad started the car and drove us to our favorite shake place.

"So how long will you be gone this time?" I asked.

"I'm hoping for just a week or two. I should be home when you get back from camp."

Dad handed me my shake and we pulled out of the drive-through. The chocolaty goodness capped off our perfect day. "I hope so. Maybe then someone will actually celebrate my birthday with me."

"Ah, your seventeenth birthday. The most magical year of your life." He winked at me.

"I thought that was a sixteenth birthday."

"Yes, well, I was a prisoner in India for your sixteenth birthday. So this year will make up for it."

I looked at him in surprise. "You didn't tell me that."

"I didn't want to ruin your birthday. Besides, I was on a top-secret mission. I couldn't tell anyone."

"So you let me think you'd just forgotten instead? Not sure that was the wisest thing to do. I was stuck with the three people who despise me the most. I had to clean our house from top to bottom so they could go to a party without me. The one good thing was that I got to sneak to the store and get my own ice cream while they were gone."

Dad's face fell. "I'm sorry about that. I'll talk to Julie for you, princess."

"Don't worry about it, Dad. It'll just make things worse. Besides, I only have one year left and I can escape." One year of abuse. My favorite. But I'd survived this long, right? "Do I get to be part of your missions after I graduate, at least?"

He glanced over at me as he pulled to a stop. "We'll see what the Order has planned. Until we know what those dreams mean, I'm not sure there's much they'll let you do."

"Stupid dreams." I took the last bite of my shake, savoring the sweetness. Who knew when I'd go out for ice cream with him again?

"I know. And it shouldn't matter. After all, no one cares about my dreams of eating pepperoni or flying."

"They might if you were eating pepperoni *while* you were flying." I climbed out of the car. "I just wish my dreams weren't so darn realistic. I wake up feeling like I've been running those stairs in real life."

Dad shook his head. "It's so bizarre. I wish I knew what we could do to stop them. No one has ever heard of this before."

"Yeah, I know. I'm just strange that way. At least my last dream was about a fair instead." I shut the door and walked to the house. The smell of lilacs filled the air. No matter how often Julie ordered me to rip the bushes out, they always seemed to grow back. They were Mom's favorite, and I had a feeling Dad had something to do with it.

"A fair? What do you mean?" Dad held on to my arm. We stood on the porch and he spoke softly so Julie wouldn't hear.

"It was one of those Renaissance fairs. I was wearing a ball dress instead of my nightgown, which was strange. Oh, and there was a fortune-teller."

He frowned. "You didn't talk to her, did you?"

My stomach clenched with fear. "Yeah. Why?"

"Could be nothing. How real was this dream?" He let go of my arm and shoved his hands in his pockets.

"Same as the stairs. The lady was creepy. I just have to stay away from fairs and ball gowns and I'll be okay, right?" I shivered, thinking of the way she had looked at me.

"I hope—" Dad cut off when the door flew open.

"Oh, sweetie pie, you're home." Julie threw her arms around him and glared at me over his shoulder. "We were getting worried about you."

Dad laughed. "It's only noon. We got home the same time we always do."

"Yes, well, I thought it might be nice for us to go boating today. At the country club. Alone." She threw another poisonous look at me before pulling back and kissing Dad soundly.

Oh, brother. That was her way of telling me to get lost. I brushed past them and went to grab some clothes so I could hop in the shower. It was quick because I knew that the shrieking and complaining would start soon—they didn't like me taking my time in the bathroom.

I got out and toweled off before noticing a note lying on the floor. Someone must have slid it under the door while I was in the shower. I picked it up and sighed at the list of chores to be done before we could leave for dinner that night. No wonder Julie had wanted to get out of the house. She needed Dad out of the way so she could force me to clean.

I dressed and opened the door, smiling brightly at Kaylee and Sarah, who were standing in front of me, hands on their hips.

"It took you long enough. We need you to get to work right now. Mom wants all this done before you leave for camp."

"I might clean the kitchen and living room, but I refuse to touch your rooms. Better hurry. Dad's taking us to dinner." I went into my room to gather my laundry so I could get started on the other chores. I kept telling myself I was doing this for my dad.

Chapter Three

"Princess, are you ready to go?" Dad called into my room.

"Uh, not really." I opened the door, yawning. The to-do list had taken forever. Kaylee and Sarah had made good and sure I was busy until the last minute.

"What happened to you?" He raised an eyebrow and pointed at my hair.

"Cleaning the oven. My ponytail got stuck on the heating element." I pulled the ponytail holder out and ran my fingers through my dark brown curls.

"Ouch. We'll wait for you. Grab a dress . . . and a brush. I'll try to keep them calm."

"Thanks, Dad." I shut the door and went back to my closet, grimacing at the clothes inside. Nothing was fit for wearing to a nice dinner. I could hear yelling out in the hallway and knew I'd better choose something quick. I took the nicest dress I had and studied it for a moment. I held my breath, focused on what I wanted, and shoved those thoughts toward the dress. I smiled at my work just as I collapsed to the floor.

The pounding on the door matched the pounding in my head. I groaned and rolled over to push myself up. Unlocking doors was one thing. Trying to make a dress look fabulous was a whole new level of magic I hadn't attempted before. I would definitely *not* be doing this to the rest of my wardrobe.

"Sydney? Is everything okay, princess?" Dad's frantic call pulled me out of my daze.

"Fine, Dad. I'll be right out." I quickly put on my new dark blue sequined dress and threw my hair up in a bun. The rings under my eyes looked terrible, but there wasn't much I could do about them. I put on some dark red lipstick and mascara before I threw open the door.

Dad stared at me in shock. "You look just like . . ." He glanced over at Julie and swallowed. "You look beautiful. Where did you get that dress?"

I smiled. "It's just something I threw together. Let's go." I walked toward the garage, smiling at the reaction from Julie and her daughters. Kaylee's mouth was wide open, and Sarah glared. Their matching form-fitting red dresses were gorgeous and would probably catch the eye of every boy there, but I had a feeling they would be demanding my dress when we got home. I wasn't allowed to look better than they did.

We piled into Dad's BMW, and I was forced to squish myself into a tiny corner so the girls wouldn't be crowded. I didn't mind. It gave me the chance to look out the window and pretend they didn't exist. The sun was beginning to set when we pulled into the parking lot of the most expensive restaurant in town.

I trailed behind the family and smiled at the glares my stepsisters kept throwing at me. I guess I'd done a better job with the dress than I'd planned. My head still throbbed from the magic I'd used. It wouldn't happen again anytime soon.

Dad gave our name to the man at the front desk, and we waited for a seat, making polite conversation. When we were led to a table, they took away the wine glasses after Dad told them we wouldn't need them, and I glanced at the menu. I ordered steak with the veggie side and took in everything going on around us. The restaurant was packed with guests eating and quietly talking. The room was dimly lit with candles on each of the tables. The deep red décor made the place feel homey. Of course, at home I didn't spend forty dollars on steak.

"So, Sydney, are you packed for tomorrow?" Julie asked, her eyes boring into my skull.

"Pretty much. I don't have a lot to pack, so I just

need my pillow and sleeping bag. Do you know if they'll have laundry rooms there?" My stomach clenched in fear. I knew what bringing this up in front of Julie would mean.

Dad laughed. "Laundry rooms? What in the world for? You're only there a week."

"I know, but I'll need to wash my pants. I only have a couple of pairs left." I ducked my head and dug in to the salad the waitress brought me.

"What do you mean? What happened to the rest of your clothes?"

I looked up at him and peeked over at Julie. "They're either too small or they have holes. I'm fine, though. I can just deal with what I have."

Julie let me know that all the time. She would insist that her girls were having a growth spurt or they were invited to a party and needed to look perfect. I didn't need anything new because according to Julie, I never went anywhere important anyway.

Dad's face turned red—something that only happens when he's super upset but doesn't want to yell. "Why haven't you gone shopping? I send you an allowance."

"You do?" I asked in surprise.

Julie stood abruptly. "I need to visit the ladies' room."

"Wait a minute." Dad took Julie's hand. "Where does Sydney's allowance go?" The calm in his voice didn't match the set to his shoulders.

"I . . . I'm saving it. For her college." She lifted her chin. "I didn't want her to go wasting it."

"Waste is buying pants she needs because her others don't fit?" Dad's normal patience was beginning to wear thin. I could see people around us taking notice.

"Dad, it's okay. We'll talk about it later, all right?" I said. It had gone silent around us.

He nodded and smiled. "Right." He took a bite of his salad, stabbing it a little harder than usual to get it on his fork.

Julie was still standing, so she picked up her purse and left for the restroom. Sarah and Kaylee hopped up and followed her, shooting me icy looks as they went.

"Dad, it's not worth making her upset. She'll only get worse when you leave." My appetite was gone. It was a shame because my steak arrived just then and it looked amazing. Maybe I could just have one bite.

"You're really out of clothes?" His eyes showed pain I hadn't seen in years.

"Yes, but it's okay. I've survived this long." I took another bite of my steak. I'd have to find another way to be depressed because this was too delicious to pass up.

"No, it's not. We'll go shopping tonight after we're done here. It's not embarrassing to go shopping with your dad, is it?"

I laughed. "Maybe a little. I don't know how many stores will be open this late, though."

"We'll make it work. I'm sorry, princess. I should be here for you more. It's not fair."

Julie and the girls returned, looking between us to try to figure out what was going on. When we didn't say anything, Julie cleared her throat and sat down, pretending like nothing had happened.

Dad and I exchanged an amused look and kept eating. We moved on to dessert and I ordered a slice of cheesecake, thoroughly enjoying it while my stepsisters and stepmom looked on in disgust.

"How can you eat something with so many calories?" Julie asked.

"Easy. I put it on my fork, stick it in my mouth, and savor every single bite." I demonstrated and smiled when I caught my dad's snicker that he instantly turned to a cough.

Julie huffed. "Well, I hope they feed you well at camp. I hate to think of the junk you'll force into yourself there. Are we quite done? I must get home. I have an awful headache coming on."

"Of course." Dad waved to let the waiter know he was ready for the check. "I'll drop you three off and then head over to the mall with Sydney."

Julie spit the water she was drinking all over the table. "What?"

"You didn't get her clothes, so I will." Dad pulled out his wallet and gave his credit card to the waiter. "That way, I can make sure her allowance goes to the right place."

"Well, I think my head is feeling better. Maybe her stepmother should go with her. Mother's touch and all that." The smile she gave me looked more like a crocodile and less like a caring mom.

I glanced over at Dad, horrified.

"No, I'll do it. I need to grab a new tablet anyway." He stood and helped Julie out of her chair and then helped Sarah and Kaylee. I was last before we headed out.

"Can I get your car, sir?" a valet asked. He smiled at me, and my heart sped up. His clear blue eyes and dimples left me breathless—which immediately made me suspicious. Why was he paying attention to me? And I could swear someone was watching me. The eerie feeling I had in my dreams was here, and I didn't like it even a little bit. The stairs were dark and creepy anyway, but the prickling on the back of my neck and the knotted feeling in my stomach always had me running faster. Only this time, I couldn't just escape, not with everyone watching. Not when I didn't know what I was running from.

Dad handed him the ticket and turned to us. He noticed my look and glanced back to where the valet had been standing. "I see you noticed Luke. He's the son of one of my partners."

"He's *gorgeous*," Sarah said. "Do you think he'd go out with me?"

Dad laughed. "Maybe so. He'll be coming to Sydney's birthday party, along with a few other young men I think you'd like. Dillon seems more your type." He gestured toward another guy coming up to the restaurant with his family.

Sarah wrinkled her nose. "No, he's more Kaylee's type. Oh! Here's Luke with the car." She hurried forward so she'd be standing in front when he opened the door.

I rolled my eyes and glanced over at Kaylee. She was too busy staring at Dillon to notice me. Sarah was right, I guess. I climbed in the other side of the car, hoping to avoid the embarrassment of Sarah throwing herself at Luke.

Dad climbed in right after. "You don't want to meet him?"

I shook my head. "No. Not right now, at least. Dad, that feeling is here. Someone's watching me, and I don't know who. What if it's Luke?"

"You felt it too, huh? There's a bad feeling here, but it's not him. His dad—" He stopped when Julie climbed in.

"Did you forget my door, Alex?" she asked, eyebrow raised.

"Oh, I'm sorry, honey. I got distracted." He waited for Kaylee and Sarah to climb in before he pulled out. He waved at Luke, and I couldn't help but notice that Luke's eyes were on me as we drove away.

Chapter Four

When we got home, I quickly changed into an old pair of denim shorts and a mint-green T-shirt before going into the office to find Dad. He was poring over books and looked up when I came in.

"I'm ready, but if you're busy, we can just stay home. It's okay, really."

He stopped what he was doing and came around the desk. "Nope, I'm good. Let's go." He locked the office door and slipped the key into his pocket. It drove Julie crazy that she could never get into the office. Dad kept it locked at all times when he was gone. There were a lot of magic books and scrolls hidden in this room that he didn't want her to see. "I'll just go tell Julie goodbye."

"'Kay. I'll be out in the car. It's unlocked, right?" I

felt my stomach drop a little at the mention of Julie. She would try again to get him to stay home, and I worried that he'd listen. Sometimes she could get him to do anything.

"Yes, it should be." Dad went to his room, and I grabbed my purse before heading toward the front door.

"We know what you're doing." Sarah stood in front of the door, arms folded. Kaylee stood next to her, filing her nails.

"What do you mean?" I asked, confused. It was Dad's idea to go shopping, not mine. I backed up as Kaylee advanced on me. One of them attacking me was bad enough. It was pure torture when they confronted me together.

"You're trying to turn your dad against our mom. It's not going to work. And you can forget about your birthday party. Mom said it won't happen."

I rolled my eyes. "I don't care what your mom says or does. Now move, please." I pushed my way between them. My heart pounded—I cared more about what her mom thought than I wanted to admit, but only out of fear. She could make my life miserable when Dad was gone. I tried to push it away, but they knew where to hit me.

"We're watching you. We know there's something wrong with you, and we're going to find out what," Kaylee hissed.

I turned back in shock, feeling like I'd been slapped. How could they know about the magic? I'd been so careful. "What do you mean?" I saw Dad coming out of his room and pleaded with him mentally to do something.

"You don't sleep. And that dress? That wasn't in your room earlier. What did you do, steal it?" She backed up when she saw Dad.

I shook my head and decided to ignore them. I ran to the car and climbed in, telling my stomach to calm down. It's not like they knew anything. Except . . . how would they know I don't sleep?

I kept silent on the drive to the mall. I only answered when Dad asked me something. Dealing with the stairs was more bearable than dealing with Kaylee, Sarah, and Julie, and that was saying something. They would know about the dress because they made sure I never had anything remotely nice in my closet. But seriously, how did they know I didn't sleep? There were the rumors at school, but those were more about my appearance than my sudden drop in grades.

We pulled into the parking lot, and Dad stopped the car. "Okay, out with it. What did they say to you?"

"Nothing. They just told me they were going to find out my secret." I rubbed my face.

"I wish them luck." His eyes flashed, but he attempted a smile to help me feel better. "They're just teenage girls, and they're jealous of their beautiful stepsister."

I rolled my eyes. "Yeah, right. But thanks for trying to cheer me up." He loved to say things like that, knowing I would squirm. I never let on how much it meant to me. It was nice hearing I was beautiful, even if it was just from my dad.

"I'll talk to Julie about them." He put his arm around me and squeezed. His familiar cologne helped calm my nerves. "Now, let's go shopping."

We separated once we got to the mall so I could find some clothes while he ran to get the tablet he needed. I tried a few different stores before I found some denim jeans and purple leggings I wanted. I found a few cute tops to go with them and then looked for clothes I could wear at camp. I tried everything on before picking out what I would buy.

Julie was the one who usually chose my clothes, so I enjoyed going through the racks on my own. There were so many styles I wanted to try, but decided to go conservative. I picked a green-and-purple pleated skirt to go with the leggings, and a loose green top to go with the jeans.

I texted Dad to let him know I was ready and went through the racks again. I stopped when I came to a dark red dress that screamed for me to get it. Dad would be there soon, but I wanted to try it on. It fit my hips and chest perfectly and showed off my dark curls. This would be perfect to wear for a dance—if I ever got asked. Dad strode into the store and pulled out his wallet just as I came out of the dressing room.

"I can put some of this back if you want. I just grabbed what I thought was cute, but I don't really need it all." Looking at the pile of clothes I'd picked out made my face burn. Now that Dad was here, I realized how carried away I'd been with finding new outfits. The dress I'd just tried on went behind my back. I could wait on this one. It wasn't something I needed, and I was embarrassed to think about getting it.

"Nice try. We'll take all of it." He went through my pile, nodding at what I'd picked out. Then he separated them into pants, shirts, and tights before looking up at me. "You don't have that much here. Are you sure you don't need a dress?"

"For what? I'm going to camp." I couldn't believe he was getting all this for me. I had to beg Julie for anything, and then work it off. I held tightly to the dress, hoping he was serious.

"Uh, church? You still do that, right?" Dad stopped laughing when he caught the look on my face. "What—you don't?"

"No. Julie won't take me. She'll go on her own, but she said I would be too distracting."

Dad ran a hand over his face. "This has got to stop. Okay, we're going to buy you dresses."

"Well, I did find this one." I pulled it out from behind me, embarrassed that I'd been hiding it. It was sad how nervous I was around him. Dad was my best friend and I told him everything. But when it came to admitting how things had been when he was gone, it was almost too much.

"Wow, princess. This is beautiful. We'll look for a few more like this. Come on." He paid for the clothes—including the dress—and we left that store. Next was a dress shop, where I quickly found some blouses in blues and reds before finding a couple of skirts. Dad insisted on two nicer dresses in green and deep purple, "just in case." I shook my head at the price tags and held the bag to me tightly. Dad whistled as we left the store, but his happiness was nowhere near what I was feeling. The old, ratty clothes I had at home could go in the garbage because I now had actual clean, nice outfits to wear. I felt like a whole new person, which was silly because they were just clothes. Maybe I wouldn't be laughed out of camp now.

I was relieved when we got home and I saw that Julie's car was gone—I wouldn't have to deal with the girls' anger when they saw my bags. I couldn't wait to pull out all the new clothes to look at them again, but I stopped short in my doorway. My room was a disaster. My posters were shredded and my blanket had been thrown into a corner in pieces. The clothes in my closet were all on the floor—except the blue dress. It wasn't anywhere.

Anger bubbled beneath the surface. I'd suffered a lot of pain to make that dress, and to think it was gone . . . Instead of exploding like I wanted to, I started cleaning. The clothes that had been scattered on the floor went in my closet, and then I pulled out the duffel bag for camp and threw in my new clothes. I'd have to buy new deodorant and toothpaste—I wasn't allowed to "mess up" Kaylee and Sarah's bathroom with my things—on the way out of town because someone had destroyed mine. But . . . why? What purpose did they have for pulling my room apart?

A shriek came from Sarah's room. "Sydney! Come here right now!"

I ran to her room, curious to see what she wanted. "What do you—" I stopped in shock. Sarah's room was torn apart even worse than mine. "What happened?"

She stood in the middle of the floor, hands clenched. "How dare you?"

"What are you talking about? I just got home. My room was trashed too."

Dad came up behind me. "What's going on, girls?" His eyes widened when he saw the mess. "I see your room was hit as well. Do you know when this would have happened? Everything was fine when we left."

"I don't know. You were taking too long shopping

41

with Sydney, so we went out for a smoothie. When we got back, we found the mess that *she* made." Sarah pointed at me, her eyes narrowed.

"Nonsense. She was with me the whole time. Clean this up and stop attacking your sister." His annoyance at their accusations was evident in his voice. He left the room, and I followed. "Someone has been through our whole house. Have you noticed anything missing?"

"My blue dress is gone, but otherwise, no. They did ruin my quilt, though." Tears welled up in my eyes. Nearly everything of my mom's had been destroyed in the space of just a couple of days. Losing another piece of her was a huge blow to me. The excitement from shopping had been shattered.

He pulled me into a hug. "I'm sorry, sweetie. Do you think you can save it?"

"Maybe. It was already a patchwork anyway. Who would do this?"

"I don't know. Maybe they thought I was too close to the cure." He pulled away, worry lines etched in his face. "I called the police after I saw my room. They should be here soon. Let's go clean up, and then we can see what can be done about the blanket."

When he opened the door to his room, I saw papers and clothes scattered across the floor. One of his paintings of an old vineyard was nothing but a shredded mess. He closed the door, drowning Julie's shrieks about her precious belongings, and I went back to my room.

Once the last of my belongings were put away, I pulled what remained of my blanket onto my bed. I was soon lost in rearranging the pieces, but then something caught my eye in the middle of the pile.

It was a black piece of cloth that was thick and rough. Wool? There was a strange feeling surrounding it, something familiar, but not in a good way. It must have been left by the intruder because no one in this house would come near this type of material. When I touched it, a sharp pain shot through my head, making me sick to my stomach at its intensity. I was yanked through darkness and transported to the stairs from my dream.

No, no, no. This wasn't supposed to happen. My head spun from being sucked in. And what was going on with my body? Was it still back at home, or was I really here? I glanced at the cloth in my hand, sure that whoever had left it in my room was here with me. I could feel them. Somewhere. I whipped around, trying to find whoever it was, my stomach clenched in fear.

"What do you want?" I screamed.

The dreams had felt real before, but this was different. I reached out to touch the wood railing and felt the roughness under my fingers. It was cold and smelled musty. I hadn't experienced it this way before. Usually, my sensations were muted, and while I climbed and woke up tired, I didn't actually feel like I was here. So did that mean my body wasn't back at home? I shook my head. No. I wouldn't freak out. There had to be a way out. I got in, right?

From all my previous searches, I knew there were no windows or doors, so like every other night, it was time to walk the stairs. I looked at the staircase below and decided the last thing I wanted to do was go down. The bad guys in horror movies are always in the basement, right? I'd gone down so many times in my dreams, but this was different. I was actually here. It was time to try going up.

I started climbing the stairs. Anything was better than just standing there. I looked ahead for any changes, expecting nothing. It was the same thing I saw every night. The same cobwebs, the same cold stone steps. The same cloak flowing around the corner . . . I stopped, my breath stuck in my throat. A cloak? There'd never been a cloak before.

I climbed faster to catch up and nearly tripped when I saw it again. The black cloak flowed behind someone just a flight ahead of me. I gasped in surprise. The material seemed to match the piece in my room. "Wait—stop!" I took the steps two at a time. My lungs began to burn and the muscles in my legs protested at the rate I was climbing, but I kept going.

"You should not be here." A deep feminine voice resounded throughout the tower.

I stopped short, hands clenched in anger. "What? I don't want to be here. Someone pulled me to this place." I looked around, trying to see who was talking. I was tired of being alone, even if it meant meeting whoever had sent me here.

Silence fell. The voice kept quiet, and I could no longer see the black cape. I sat down in defeat, feeling more alone than ever before. I just wanted to go home. Usually I had to wake up to get out of here. Wait—wake up! I shook my head, annoyed that I hadn't thought of it before. I pinched myself hard, but nothing happened.

I needed a bigger jolt. I looked down at the stairs and grimaced. There was another way to do it, but it wouldn't be very fun. Sadly, I had no other choice. I lay down on the top step and rolled forward, hitting the step below. It jarred, and I could feel the uneven steps dig into my arm. I rolled again and smacked my head on the next one, making the headache I'd felt earlier seem like nothing. I kept going, crying out as I fell.

And landed on my bed. I groaned, holding my pounding head, then pulled myself up and looked around the room. Everything seemed the same, and only minutes had passed. I stared down at the cloth near my hand. It did match the cloak I'd seen on the stairs. That meant whoever it was had been in my room. I stood and walked around, trying to shake the dream.

I heard a knock. "Come in!"

Dad opened the door. "Well, we solved the case of the missing dress, at least." He held it out. It was still in perfect shape, so it hadn't been found by whoever had broken in.

"Where was it?" I took it and hugged it to me, then hung it up in the closet. It was surprising that it hadn't been destroyed along with everything else.

"Sarah had it. I happened to find it when she was ranting about unfair shopping trips."

He picked up a few pieces of my blanket and smoothed them out.

"No!" I dove forward just as he reached for the black piece of cloak. "Don't touch this." I grabbed a bag from our shopping trip and used it over my hand like a glove to pick up the fabric. "This just sent me to the dream world."

He jerked his hand back and wiped it on his pant leg. "How? Where did it come from?" Carefully taking the bag from me, he put it in his pocket.

I shrugged and sat on the bed next to him. "I don't know. I'm assuming from whoever broke into our house."

"I'm going to keep this with me. You may have run across a good piece of evidence." He looked closer at me. "Where did you get this bruise?" He pointed to my arm.

"What do you mean?" I was surprised to find a large ugly purple blotch on my skin. "It must have been from falling down the stairs."

"You fell down the stairs?" He checked my arm again. "Are you hurt anywhere else?"

"Yeah, I smacked my head." I reached up and found a large goose egg where there hadn't been one before. "I had to wake myself up somehow. But I don't understand how I'm bruised in real life when it happened in a dream."

He stood. "I think I need to move my trip up—this can't keep happening. I'll see you off to camp tomorrow and then I'd better leave." He bent over and kissed me on the forehead. "You'll be okay at camp?"

"Away from Julie and her monsters? Yes."

He lifted an eyebrow. "Monsters? Talk nicer, please." He went to the door. "Oh, and I'm getting a different lock for your room while you're gone. You paid a huge price for that dress—not how I would have advised you to use your magic, but it's good to see you practicing. Night, honey."

"Night, Dad." I picked up all the pieces of my blanket and set them in the chest at the end of my bed. After checking one more time to be sure I had everything packed for camp, I went and found another toothbrush and toothpaste to brush my teeth. I had to sneak into the crawlspace storage area to get them so Julie wouldn't find out. She was very picky about how often I replaced anything, and she'd just given me a toothbrush a couple of weeks before.

Once my teeth were brushed, I sneaked back to my room and climbed into bed. I said a quick little prayer of thanks for my dad and what he'd given me, and then pulled out a book to read. I wanted to stay awake as long as possible—I wasn't looking forward to going back to the stairs.

Chapter Five

I took one last look at my room before hefting my bag up on my shoulder. I really hoped Dad would lock my door and hide the key because I had noticed Sarah eyeing my closet earlier that morning.

It was a two-hour trip to camp, so I had loaded my bag with books. There was no way I wanted to fall asleep on a bus full of other people—if I screamed out in my dreams, I'd never hear the end of it.

I waved at Sarah and Kaylee before climbing into Dad's BMW. They didn't have to know that the smile on my face was because I was free of them for a week. Julie sulked and refused to wave as we pulled away, but I was totally okay with that.

"There are a few things you need to know before you head off to camp," Dad started.

"I won't go near boys, Dad." I watched out the window as we passed by the businesses in town. I waved at a group of girls from my class standing in front of an ice cream shop and smiled when they actually waved back.

Dad laughed. "That's not what I was going to say. And it would be nice if you actually did meet a boy. What I meant was that you need to watch out for anyone acting suspicious. I, uh, have a few enemies out there, and they'd stop at nothing to see me go down."

"Oh, great. I'm going to magic camp. Who *won't* be acting suspicious?" I threw my hands up, but inside, I was bouncing with excitement. I would be around other kids with magic for the first time in my life. Having a little danger added to the mix just made it sound more intriguing.

"Fair enough, but you'll know what I mean by suspicious. Most of these kids will still be learning how to control their magic, just like you. They will still feel the pain of using it. Watch for those who can use their powers with no consequences."

"But how is that possible? Everyone feels pain."

"Those who have studied magic for years can keep themselves from feeling it." He clenched his jaw. "Maybe this wasn't such a good idea."

"Dad, I'll be fine. I know how to take care of myself. I've done it for years." I caught his wince and immediately felt guilty. "Sorry, Dad. I know you'd be home if you could. But my point is that I can watch out for these people on my own."

He slowed down for a truck that had pulled onto the highway. "I want you to text me the second you find anything suspicious. Got it?"

"Of course. Unless there's no signal."

He pointed to the dash. "I put a satellite phone in there. You'll be able to contact me from anywhere."

"Even on the stairs?" I pulled a small phone from the glove compartment and studied it. I could take pictures with it, but otherwise, it was pretty simple.

"That's the one thing I don't know. Since you're the only person who seems to have these dreams, we can't test that. So . . . just stay away from them, okay?" He glanced over and smiled at me.

"Got it. Of course, if I knew how to do that . . ." I had somehow managed to stay away from the stairs the night before, but the dreams had still been disturbing. I was at a ball, rushing away from someone or something. I'd bolted out of bed before I could find out who or what it was.

Dad's cell phone rang, and he answered it, leaving me to my thoughts. He was still making his travel arrangements when we pulled into a parking lot next to an old cabin. He helped me grab my bag and kissed me on the cheek with a whispered "I love you. Good luck!" and climbed back into his car.

I sighed and went over to the check-in by myself. After making sure they had my name right, I picked up the registration packet and handed off my luggage. We would be catching a bus from there to the camp. Everyone else had someone to talk to, so I found a place to sit by myself until it was time to leave.

A few minutes later, Dad left his car and ran over to me. "Sorry about that. The arrangements are made, and I'll be flying out in just a few hours. I have a spa day scheduled for Julie and the girls so they'll be more understanding when I take off."

"So if you're leaving, how will you help me if I'm in trouble?" I asked, picking at the threads on my bag.

"I have a few friends who'll be around, keeping an eye on you. You'll be fine." He kissed me on the forehead just as the director announced it was time to load up. "Good luck, princess. Remember who you are, and know your mom is watching over you." He pulled me into a hug.

"Thanks, Dad. I love you." I kissed him on the cheek and ran to the bus. I would miss him, but the thought of finally being around others with magic was exciting. I found a seat no one had taken and dropped into it. Dad stood with his hands in his pockets, waiting for us to leave. I waved at him through the window to let him know where I was. He brightened and waved back.

"Is this seat taken?" a girl's voice asked.

I looked up to see a thin girl with long brown hair staring down at me, biting her lip. Her floral peasant skirt clashed with the stripes on her blouse.

"Nope. You can sit here." I scooted over so she had room.

"I'm Jade," she said.

I looked over at her. "I'm Sydney." I had no idea what else to say. People didn't usually talk to me.

"This is my second year. My mom is one of the instructors. How about you?" She pulled her hair back and put it into a ponytail.

"Nope, this is my first year." I paused. "I didn't even know they had these camps. I usually just teach myself."

"You teach yourself?" she asked, eyebrows raised. "Isn't that dangerous?"

I shrugged. If it was, I had no idea. I'd never known anyone else with magic except for Dad. "Maybe. It's never caused problems before. I don't use it very often—my stepsisters and stepmom don't know we have magic. I'd prefer they never find out." I clamped my mouth shut. I was so excited to have someone to talk to, I couldn't help but tell her everything.

Jade made a face. "Ugh, that sounds awful." She smiled again. "Well, you'll learn all kinds of magic here. And the best part is the competition the last day of camp."

My stomach tied in knots. "There's a competition? I hadn't heard about that. What are we supposed to do?"

"It's in the packet." She reached into her bag and handed me some papers. "We'll be doing archery, dueling, and a few different sports. Every year, it's a different theme. Whoever wins between us and the other camp plans it for the next year."

I read through the papers. "I can't believe my dad didn't tell me about this—I don't how to do any of those things." Knowing Dad, he most likely kept it a secret so I wouldn't stress out. He was always trying to protect me, but it didn't always work out like he hoped.

She shoved the papers back in her bag, grabbed a package of gum, and put some in her mouth before offering me a piece.

"Thanks." I took it from her. "So, is camp fun?"

Jade grinned. "Yes. 'Camping' doesn't begin to describe what we do there. We stay in cabins, and part of our job is to decorate our rooms however we want. We get some pretty wild designs."

"So, do we just build off what other people did before us?" I would have to come up with something original.

"No, they set it all back to plain old cabins when camp is over. I guess other groups come here after us. We wouldn't want to spoil it for them." She leaned back and blew a bubble, allowing it to pop in her face.

"How did you decorate yours last year?" I asked, hoping for ideas.

"I went retro, and I'll probably do the same thing this year. If you couldn't tell by my clothes, I love the hippie movement. What are you going to do?"

I thought for a moment. What did I even like? I was too busy pleasing Julie to come up with my own hobbies. "I don't know. My room is pretty simple at home."

She waved her hand. "Just forget about your room at home. What do you *want* it to look like?"

"I'd have a castle, of course." I smiled. *One I didn't have to clean.* "With thick carpets and fluffy blankets."

She raised her eyebrows. "Seriously? I wouldn't take you for a girly-girl."

"I'm not. Who knows—maybe that's why I want it that way." Or maybe I was exhausted and just wanted a good long nap in a huge bed with lots of pillows.

"I guess that works." Jade glanced out the window. "Oh! It looks like we're here." She grabbed her bag and zipped it up, waiting for the bus to stop.

I watched in awe as we pulled in. The cabins were surrounded by tall pine trees and nestled against a small, peaceful lake. In the center was a large cabin with a field next to it. The flagpole in the center held an American flag, and below that flew the camp flag. It was bright yellow, with "Enchanted Acres" scrawled across the top and a castle beneath.

Jade looked at the flag in disgust. "We really need to update that. It's way out of touch." She glanced over at me. "Although, I guess that would go with your design ideas, wouldn't it?"

"I guess so." I followed her off the bus. "Do we have any free time to do what we want? Or are we in classes the whole time?"

"Yeah, that's part of the competition on the last day." Jade stood on her tiptoes, scanning the crowd, apparently looking for someone before grabbing my hand. "Come on. Let's get checked in together so we can be in the same cabin." She yanked me through the crowds until we came up to an adult version of Jade. "Hey, Mom. This is Sydney. She's going to room with me, okay?"

I could feel my face heat up, and Jade's mom studied me before smiling brightly. I wasn't used to people wanting to hang out with me, let alone wanting to share a cabin. Dad would be proud I made a friend on the first day.

"Welcome, Sydney. I'm Sheri. It's nice to meet you." She shook my hand and then looked down at her clipboard. "You two girls will be in cabin seven. You'll find a key and all your bedding in there. Jade, don't forget that you're helping with arts and crafts later today."

"I won't. Come on, Sydney." Jade pulled me through the rest of the crowd before letting go of my hand and leading the way to the cabin.

As we rounded the lake, I glanced into the water

and gasped. A bright turquoise tail covered in scales flipped out of the water. "Is that a mermaid?"

"Of course. They need to learn their magic too. This is their first year here. After camp, they'll go back down into the depths of the ocean. They won't really interact with us at all." She stopped in front of a cabin with a large seven next to the door. "This is where I stayed last year. Hopefully we have all the same roommates. It was one big party."

I sighed. Great—everyone would know each other, and I would be left out yet again. I waited by the door and listened to squeals and excitement when the four girls saw Jade. The front room had a few worn couches with a yellow shag rug on the floor between them. The walls were sparsely decorated with mountain scenes.

"Girls, meet Sydney. She's new this year." Jade pulled me farther in to the room.

"Hey, Sydney. I'm Ashley." A tall girl with bright blue eyes and brown hair nodded toward me.

I nodded back. "Hi. It's nice to meet you."

"Heidi." A short, bouncy girl came bounding up to me, chewing bubble gum. Her button nose and mischievous eyes made her look younger than the other girls.

"Katy." A girl with long brown hair waved and smiled. She was on the floor, stretching in a position that made me hurt just thinking about it. "Sorry—I'm getting ready for my dance class."

There are dance classes here? I couldn't believe how much was available. I'd have to find the schedule and study it.

"She says that, but she's usually in that position." A tall girl with red hair held out her hand. "I'm Liz. Your room is down the hallway to the right. I suppose Jade told you we'll be decorating it later?"

"Yeah, she did. Thanks." I went to find my room. It was small, with a bed, a dresser, and a few paintings of wildflowers. The window above the dresser was open and let in a cool breeze. I moved over to it and looked out—I had a great view of the mountainside. There was a squirrel up in the tree, and a deer in the distance.

A chill suddenly ran down my spine. Someone was out there—someone in a cloak. He stood there, unmoving, out in the woods. I backed away from the window and pulled down the blinds. I shook my head, trying to brush away the fear. I'd only been here for a few minutes—there couldn't be anyone after me already. Maybe it was someone getting ready for an acting class or something, but the way my legs were shaking, I knew I didn't want to find out.

Chapter Six

I grabbed one of my books and went out to the living room, trying to find some kind of distraction. All the girls were still there, chatting about boys. Katy stood up from doing the splits and sat on the couch.

"Oh, you're back. Do you like your room?" Liz asked.

"It's small, but I love it." I plopped down on the couch next to Jade.

Ashley looked up from painting her nails. "Just wait until you get to redecorate." She blew on her fingers before starting on the other hand.

I put my feet up on the coffee table and opened my book to read, but just then, I heard a bell clanging loudly outside. The girls jumped up, and Ashley put away her nail polish.

"Lunchtime. I was wondering when they'd call us—I'm starving." Jade was the first one to the door. "You coming, Sydney?"

"Yep, let's go."

The six of us walked to the lodge together. Inside, the dining room was packed with tables full of campers. The serving area was in the back, and the line trailed toward the door we'd just come through. My roommates giggled, and I was surprised when they all turned to me. "What?"

Liz giggled again and nodded toward a table of boys. "You didn't notice the guy looking at you? His eyes followed you all the way in here."

I glanced over and was surprised to see Luke sitting there, smiling at me. He was here? I mean, I guess if my dad knew him, that would make sense. "Oh, that guy. Dad introduced us last night." I smiled back at him and turned away before he could see my red face.

"You know him?" Jade shrieked. "He's the guy everyone dies over every year."

"I didn't actually talk to him. Dad just pointed him out." I didn't want to add that I had avoided him because of my stepsisters.

"Yes, well, it seems like you made quite an impression." Heidi grinned.

I grabbed my food tray and then followed Jade to a seat. It was strange to be sitting next to friends—usually I was on my own in a corner.

Katy took a bite of her burger. "Man, this is way better than school lunch."

Ashley shoved a couple of fries in her mouth, followed by lemonade. "I'd have to agree with you there."

"Ew, Ashley. At least chew them up first." Heidi threw a fry at her before leaning forward. "Sydney, he's still watching you."

I turned and caught Luke's eye just as he looked down at his food. What was up with him? And how much did Dad actually know about him? I figured I'd better call him later and ask. I glanced over to see that the girls were looking at me expectantly. The last thing they'd want to hear was that I thought he was suspicious, so I blurted out the first thing that came to mind. "He's cute, isn't he?" I was relieved when they all burst into giggles.

"I'm pretty sure he's the cutest guy here," Liz said, blushing. "Although Max isn't so bad either." She nodded toward another table, where a boy with dark hair sat eating quietly.

"You always go for the shy ones," Heidi remarked. "I think I want Blake over there."

The girls went on and on about which guys they wanted, but I lost track as my mind drifted. It was screaming for sleep—something I wasn't about to let it have. I picked at my green beans and jumped when the other girls stood. All the campers headed out of the lodge, so I followed, completely oblivious to where we were going next.

"Hey, Sydney!" a voice called from behind me.

I turned in surprise, then stopped and waited for Luke to catch up. "Yeah?"

"I just wondered what class you're going to." His dimpled smile made my knees weak, and I had to remind myself to talk. Or breathe.

"I . . . actually don't know. I wasn't paying attention when the others decided." I looked around for them. "And now I've lost them."

Luke laughed. "They went toward your cabin."

"And how do you know which one is my cabin?" I smiled, but inside, I was at war with myself, trying to decide if I should be worried. I was tired of always feeling threatened.

It was his turn to blush. "I might have asked Sheri after I saw you and Jade talking to her."

"Am I really that interesting?" I took a small step back. My mind drifted to the person in the woods. Was Luke the one watching my cabin? Part of me wanted to run as fast as I could, but the other part wanted to stick around.

"Yes, you are. Plus, your dad asked me to keep an eye out for you." He shoved his hands in his pockets.

"Oh." I was surprised at my disappointment. At first, I was scared that he was following me, and then suddenly, I was depressed that he was only following me because of my dad. I would never figure guys out. Or myself, for that matter. My thoughts must have shown on my face because he reached out his hand to stop me from walking away.

"Look, it's not just because of your dad. When I saw you at dinner last night, I wanted to get to know you better. I just figured now was a good time."

"Oh." I kicked myself mentally. That's all I could say? "So, what class are you going to?"

He shrugged. "I was thinking of practicing some archery."

"We can do whatever we want? Don't we have somewhere to be?" I really needed to look at my packet.

"We will tomorrow. Today is just getting to know the camp. Want to come with me?"

"I . . ." If Dad had sent him to watch me, there wasn't a safer place for me to be than with him, right? "Sure. I should probably tell my friends, though."

"I'll come with you. I mean, if that's okay with you."

"Of course. But don't you have friends to hang out with?" We started toward my cabin.

"They all went for a swim." He motioned toward the lake.

I stared at the lake for a moment. The calm water I'd seen earlier was disturbed by the ripples that flowed out from the kids who were swimming. "Have you seen mermaids before?"

He shook his head. "No. I was really surprised to see them. It's partly why I didn't go swimming."

"You're scared of mermaids?" I teased.

He laughed. "No. But it's still strange to me. I'll get used to it." He stopped, and I suddenly realized we were in front of my cabin.

I ran up the stairs and opened the door to let Katy know where I'd be, and slammed the door shut before Luke could hear the squeals that erupted inside.

I enjoyed the summer day as we walked in silence toward the archery field. The sun was warm, but the cool breeze kept me from getting too hot. The smell of pines cleansed the worries that had plagued me for as long as I could remember. Animals in the woods surrounding the camp scurried about, ignoring the campers nearby.

"Earlier today, I could have sworn I saw someone with a cloak in the woods," I blurted out.

Luke stiffened. "What? Where?"

I pointed behind my cabin. "Out there somewhere. I didn't see him for long. It could have been my imagination."

Luke strode toward the back of the cabins and did a search. "Everything seems fine. No footprints," he muttered to himself.

"What are you talking about? I told you it could have been my imagination."

"Yeah, maybe. Did they come close?" he asked.

"No, they were clear out there. Really, it wasn't that big of a deal." The way Luke reacted had me more worried than anything else did.

He checked the woods one more time before heading toward the front of the cabins, and then we continued on. He pulled out his phone and typed for a minute before slipping it back in his pocket.

"I thought we didn't get a signal out here."

"Most people don't, but I assume you have the same kind of phone I have."

Wait—how did he know about the phones? And if he had one . . . I stopped and faced him. "Who are you?"

"Our dads work together, and I've been sent to watch over you. Otherwise, I'm just a normal guy wanting to hang out with a beautiful girl—and teach her how to shoot arrows."

My face burned. He'd called me beautiful! "I thought you said you were going there to *practice* archery."

"I said that. But what I really meant was that I was going to beat everyone there." His mischievous grin had my heart beating rapidly.

I stepped in front of him, hands on my hips. "I see how you are. I'll watch you this time, but then I challenge you to a game of baseball."

"Ah, baseball, huh? I have a feeling you'll beat me there. Maybe we should go for something we're both bad at. Like canoeing."

"Hey, who said I was bad at canoeing?"

"Well, can you actually do it?"

I peeked over at the canoes. "Well, no, but that's beside the point."

Luke chuckled as he picked out a bow for himself and then helped me choose one. We went over to the targets, and Luke demonstrated how to use the bow.

I was thankful I had built up muscle going to the batting cages because I needed it to help me pull back on the bowstring. I let the first arrow loose, and it didn't go anywhere near the target. I watched Luke shoot a few times—hitting near the bull's-eye each time—before I tried again.

I missed the target when Luke stood close to me and helped get everything in the correct position. My arms were where they should be, but inside, my brain and heart were going wild. I'd never had a boy this close to me before, and I fully enjoyed every second of it.

He helped me get the arrow where it needed to be and then stepped back. I shot and hit near the center of the target.

"Hey, that's much better. But then, my teaching skills *are* pretty amazing."

"Yes, they are. I mean, um, thanks." I tried one more arrow, and this time it came even closer. "Wow, never thought I'd do that well. Of course, I never imagined I'd be shooting a bow in the first place."

Luke took my bow from me and set both of them by a haystack, and we went in search of the arrows. His were easy because they were all on the target. We had looked for about ten minutes before I finally spotted my last one. We took everything back, set it with the other equipment, and walked toward my cabin.

"So, what do we want to do next?" Luke asked.

"Baseball?" I was dying to see the field. Plus, it would help me relax. I kicked a stone, watching it roll toward the lake and land with a splash.

"Ah, see, that requires more than just the two of us." He took a step ahead of me and walked backwards. "You sure you want that?"

"Hey, we did your thing. Now it's time for mine. Or are you afraid you'll lose?" I asked, grinning. I waved at Heidi and Ashley as they jogged past. In the distance, other campers were practicing magic by making fireballs in their hands. I couldn't imagine the control it would take to do that.

"Oh, you're on. You find a team and I'll find a team and we'll meet on the field at—" He checked his watch. "Four o' clock. Does that work?"

I looked down at my watch, surprised that two hours had already passed since lunch. "Deal. I'll see you then." I waved, ran up the steps to my cabin, and turned back to watch him leave, hands in his pockets.

Chapter Seven

"So . . . *someone* was gone for a really long time." Jade stood by the door, her arms folded and eyebrows raised.

"We were practicing archery. It takes a while." I went past all the staring girls and into my room. A glance in the mirror showed my flushed cheeks. Maybe it was the sunshine, but I was pretty sure it was the cute boy who had just chosen to hang out with me. I flopped on my bed, thinking of how it felt to have him so near. I pulled out my phone and sent a text to my dad, thanking him for sending Luke to watch over me, and then went back to daydreaming.

Someone knocked, and I opened the door to find all five girls standing there, smiling. Ashley grabbed my hand and pulled me back out to the couch.

"Okay, spill. How did you do that?" Katy asked.

"Do what?" I asked, surprised.

"You're here for four hours, and you get the guy everyone's wanted for years."

"I told you at lunch—he knows my dad. Or, I guess his dad knows my dad. Apparently, my dad asked him to keep an eye on me. Nothing more."

They stared at me for a second before bursting into laughter. I waited for them to get done so I could figure out what the big joke was.

"Come on, Syd. Surely you're not *that* blind. That may have been what happened, but it's obvious he likes you," Liz said, still laughing.

"What are you talking about?" I was surprised at the nickname. No one but Amy had ever called me "Syd," and we'd been friends for years.

"We haven't seen him smile at anyone like that before. And believe me, we know. Everyone watches him," Heidi said.

He *liked* me? I mean, I wanted him to, but to think he actually might . . . "Uh, creepy. He's just a guy." I suddenly remembered what I was supposed to be doing. "Oh! Do you guys want to play baseball with me at four? I kinda challenged him to a game, and I need a team."

"Baseball? As, in sports?" Jade asked. "Will boys be there?"

I laughed. "Yes. Or at least, I assume so. I doubt Luke will get a team of girls together. Please? I don't know anyone else." I bit my lip, hoping they wouldn't say no. I didn't want to have to tell Luke that I had no other friends.

They looked at each other before turning back to me. Ashley grinned. "Let's do it. We'll just have to borrow some mitts. I have one, but the others don't."

I breathed out in relief. "Thanks, girls. Let's go find some mitts." I went to my room to grab mine from my bag and pulled my hair up into a ponytail. Liz and Heidi were out on the couches when I left the room, and we were met by the other girls a few minutes later.

"We'll have to be done by five for my class," Katy said.

"That's okay. I want to be showered before dinner anyway." I didn't want to admit that I was hoping Luke would want to sit by me.

We headed to the lodge to check out the sports equipment and then went to the field to practice catching before the other team got there. Liz and Ashley had found a few extra players on our way over, and I was pretty impressed by how well we played together.

A few minutes later, the boys showed up. I knew that without looking from the way the girls all straightened up and touched their hair. I turned and walked over to Luke.

"Ready to lose?" I cringed. Why was I talking like this? I never talked to boys, let alone teased them.

"To you? I can think of worse things." He winked. "So, do we want to mix these teams up, or do we want girls against guys?"

I turned. "What do you think, girls?"

"They have more players than we do. Maybe we should mix it up." Katy had come to stand by me. "You and Luke can be the team captains."

"Fair enough. Luke, why don't you start?" I was shaking with nervousness.

We took turns picking people, and after a game of rock, paper, scissors, Luke's team went out to the field and my team got ready to bat.

"Okay, team, let's line up." A tall boy with dark hair and glasses stood up in front.

"Hey, this is Sydney's team," Liz said from the bench.

"Yeah, well, I'm in charge now. I'll bat first." He looked over at me and smirked. He looked . . . familiar somehow.

I stared at him, trying to figure out how I knew him. He must have taken my silence as giving in, because he smiled and grabbed a bat. All the confidence drained out of me as a sense of uneasiness settled in. I sighed and sat down at the end of the bench.

"Wait." Heidi jumped up and got up in the guy's face. "Look, Nick. I don't know who you think you are. This is *her* team. You will let her choose who goes where." It was comical, with her standing a good six inches shorter than Nick, but he stepped back. Wow, she could be scary when she wanted to be.

He looked over at me and glared before bowing. "Okay, Your Highness. Who would you like to bat first?"

I flinched. His glare was like Sarah's when she didn't get her way. "Um, go ahead since you're ready." I stood and looked at the lineup. "Let's alternate boys and girls so it's a little more fair for this first inning. Then I'll rearrange things as we go."

"Whatever." Nick went out to home plate, and I helped get everyone in their batting order before collapsing on the bench.

That was way too confrontational for someone who had tried not to care for so long. The look in his eye let me know I didn't want to mess with him.

Heidi leaned around Max. "You okay? You look pale."

"I'm fine. Thanks for sticking up for me. I'm . . . not used to that."

"You're not used to jerks?"

I lived with three of them. I'd learned to avoid them. "No, people sticking up for me."

"Well, that's what I'm here for." She turned to watch the game.

Nick made it to first base, and Liz was up to bat. I rolled my eyes when I saw the guys move in. Typical. The pitcher threw some wild pitches and Liz walked. I noticed that he did that with the next couple of girls, and my blood boiled.

Peter and Max got out and the bases were filled when it was my turn. Heidi gave me a thumbs-up from first base. "You got this!"

The pitcher threw a low, fast pitch and I held out through that one and the next. The third came perfectly and I hit the ball with everything I had, smiling as I ran the bases and slid into home. My team cheered wildly while Luke's team just stared, not knowing what had just happened. Nick got out on the next play, and it was our turn to take the field.

The game heated up after that, and we were ahead by three by the time five o'clock came around and Katy had to leave to teach her class. We wandered off the field, and Luke caught up to me.

"You weren't kidding when you said you liked baseball."

"Nope. Dad and I go to the batting cages whenever he's home." I hadn't heard from Dad since I texted. I wondered if he was okay.

"That would explain the home runs. Hey, I need to catch up to the guys. See you at dinner?"

"Sounds good." I waved and continued to my cabin, giddy. He wanted to see me again! I would have a chance to show off my new clothes. I hurried to my room and threw my mitt on the bed before taking a quick shower. I put on my purple leggings, plaid skirt, and green top, making sure everything matched. Once everyone else was ready, we headed out to the lodge for dinner. Katy would meet us there.

Clouds were piling up and heading our direction. The wind had picked up too. We hurried into the dining hall and straightened each other's hair while we stood in line. I searched the tables for Luke, but didn't see him. I pushed away my disappointment and picked up my tray before going over to sit with Jade and the rest of my friends.

Lightning crashed outside and I watched the rain pour down, hoping I would see Luke come in soon. Instead of going back to our cabins, we helped clean up dinner and then pushed all the tables against the walls. Music blasted through the speakers, and the counselors pulled out board games.

I half-heartedly moved my chess piece while I watched the door. After losing to Jade, I stood and went to the window. I couldn't see the nearest cabins because of the rain. Frustrated about dumb boys and their need to mess with my head, I turned away, but whipped back around when I caught movement outside the window.

Luke came in, drenched. He went over and talked to the cooks, and they gave him a plate of food. He scanned the room before heading in my direction.

"Would you like me to find you a towel?" Jade asked.

"That would be great. Thanks." He sat on the floor by my feet.

I slid onto the floor next to him. "Where were you?"

He shoveled food into his mouth and held up a finger. "I've been on the phone. You and I need to talk whenever we can leave here," he said when he'd swallowed the bite.

My heart plummeted down to my sneakers. "What's going on?"

He glanced at me between bites. "Who said anything was wrong?"

"You can't just tell me we need to talk and assume I won't think something's up. What's going on?"

"I promise, you want to wait until no one else is around." He shoved another bite in his mouth. "Now, you can come out into the storm with me so we can talk, or we can wait here and you can agonize over what I'm going to say. But I'd rather get it over with, if it's okay with you."

His blue eyes searched mine, and I knew something was wrong. Very wrong. I nodded once. "Good thing I didn't spend much time on my hair. Let's go."

I went over to where Jade was playing a game with Heidi and Ashley and let them know I was leaving.

"Are you crazy? You can't go out in that!" Heidi gestured toward the rain. "You'll get drenched."

"Not to mention going off with a guy you only met today."

"I went off with him earlier and I survived. I'll be back at the cabin as soon as I can." I waved to them and met Luke at the door.

We waited to make sure there were no counselors nearby and then darted out into the rain. I felt like a bucket of water had been thrown over my head. I was soaked through within seconds as we ran toward the outer part of the camp.

Luke stopped and turned toward me. "I'm sorry to bring you out here, but I couldn't let anyone else hear what's going on."

I tried to suppress my shivering, but it was no use. "Is it my dad?"

He nodded. "Apparently, when he was showing the cloth you found in your room to my dad and a few other members of the Order, his hand brushed against the fabric and he fell to the ground. They can't wake him up. He'll groan and mutter your name, but that's it."

My heart shattered. I covered my face with my hands and started sobbing. I'd been warned that if I didn't stay away from the stairs, I'd lose what I loved most. Nothing mattered more to me than my dad. And I knew where he was—he was on those stairs. But would he be able to get back out, like I could?

Luke's strong arms came around me and hugged me

close to him. "I'm sorry. I was on the phone so long because we were trying to find out who his contacts are, to see if they're any closer to finding your cure."

I shook my head. "He's looked for cures for years. They supposedly found one that he was supposed to go get this week." I was glad it was raining at that moment, as my tears mixed in with the rain. "The only thing we can do is hope that I can get into the dream and find him."

He pulled back and tilted my chin up so I was looking into his eyes. "You can't—it's too dangerous. We'll get your dad back—we have to. He's the key to helping you, and he's . . ." He paused. ". . . important to us."

I was sure he was about to say something else, but let it go. "I'll do whatever it takes to get him back. I hope you realize that. Not doing anything isn't okay with me." I wiped my eyes—not that it would do any good in this rain.

He put his arm around me and guided me back to the cabins. "I don't blame you. But please be smart."

"I will be. I need him, Luke. He's the only good thing in my life."

He took my hand and looked into my eyes. "I hope you can find other good things too. Please don't worry. We'll make sure your dad wakes up."

"Thanks, Luke." I looked around and noticed the

rain was slowing. "Please let me know if you hear anything, okay?" I pulled away and started to trudge to my cabin.

"Sydney, wait!" Luke grabbed my arm. "Please don't do anything crazy."

"I won't. I just need to be alone." I went into my cabin and took off my muddy sneakers by the door before going to my room to change. I put on pajamas and a robe before taking all my wet clothes to the bathroom to hang them up.

There was only one person who could help my dad, and it was me. I locked my bedroom door, hoping none of my roommates would be getting back any time soon. I needed to find Dad on the stairs, and I didn't want to be interrupted. It wouldn't be hard for me to fall asleep. I was exhausted after just the first day here.

Chapter Eight

I stood in the middle of the staircase. This was the first time I had ever been happy to see this place. I turned in circles, trying to decide which way I should go. My dress brushed against the steps. Ugh, back in the dress again.

I picked up the skirts and began climbing. "Dad?" I called, and then laughed to myself. Of course he wouldn't answer. That would be too easy. I ran upstairs, hoping for any sort of change in the stairs, but I should have known better. They never changed.

Suddenly, I heard a noise from above, and I started running faster. A door! I reached it, breathing heavily, and grasped the handle. The door was heavy, and I struggled to open it. Inside was a brightly lit room, and I had to shield my eyes. The walls were stone and covered with cobwebs, like the stairs. It wasn't furnished except for the dais in the center. It reminded me of the bed in the story of Snow White, except that it was Dad who lay on it, not moving. I ran forward and grabbed his hand.

"Dad? Dad? Are you okay?" I tried to wake him by patting his cheek and shaking his shoulder, but nothing worked. "Come on, wake up!"

"He won't awaken."

I jerked and whipped around to find the woman from the fair I'd dreamed about a few days before.

"What do you mean? And why is he asleep? I don't fall asleep when I come here." I kept hold of my dad's hand, hoping he wouldn't disappear. It was a relief that his skin was still warm.

"This is part of your curse, not his. By coming into this dream, he has destroyed all chances of saving either of you."

I rocked back on my heels, breathless. Curse? I swallowed. This woman could have the answers we'd been looking for. "What do you mean?"

"The curse. You didn't think you came here every night just for exercise, did you? And I warn you not to throw yourself down the stairs again." She looked at me sternly.

"Yeah, I learned my lesson. I still hurt from that one. But who cursed me? And why?"

The woman stared at me. "Your mother wanted you more than anything. She was willing to pay whatever price she must for a princess she could love and raise, and made a bargain with an evil woman to get what she wanted. However, she died before she could free herself from the promise she'd made. You, in turn, must find a way to break the curse."

"But how does that even work?" My head wouldn't stop trying to explode.

"She found what the woman wanted in exchange, but for some reason, you remain here. You must find a way to escape and destroy this place, or the woman will have power over you forever."

I growled in frustration. "I've tried. Every night, I run these stairs and I get nowhere. Every day, I fight overwhelming exhaustion because I get no rest. If I'm supposed to stop this, shouldn't something change?"

"But your dreams have changed, have they not?"

"I suppose . . . yes."

She grinned. "Well, then, princess, I suggest you run." She waved her hands and disappeared from the room.

I woke to knocking and yelling outside my door. The clock showed that two hours had passed since I'd gone to sleep.

"Just a second!" I jumped out of bed and stretched before going to the door and opening it a crack.

"Where were you?" Jade demanded.

"Asleep. What's going on?"

"You know what I mean. We couldn't find you for hours." Her wild eyes made me take a step back.

"He had to tell me about my dad." My eyes watered, threatening to spill over.

She leaned forward. "Wait—what about your dad?"

"He's cursed. He was sent into a dream state, and

now he can't wake up. I came back here to sleep and see if I could figure things out."

"He's cursed, and you came home to take a nap? How does that help anything?" Her eyebrows scrunched together.

"It's hard to explain. He's cursed because of me. I thought I could get some answers from my dreams." I opened the door farther to let her in.

"Whoa, are you a seer?" she asked, sitting down on the floor.

I shook my head. How could I explain this? I sat for a moment, wondering if I trusted her. So far, she'd been nothing but nice. Keeping everything to myself was tiring, though. I'd take the chance. "No, it's not like that. I've had these nightmares for years, and he got pulled into them. The only problem is, he can't get out like I can." I ran my fingers through my hair in frustration.

"What kind of nightmares? I have a dream interpretation book. Maybe that will help."

I laughed. "Oh, believe me, we've tried everything. Today I learned I'm cursed. Well, my mom was cursed, and I'm still paying for it."

"Wow. So, what's this dream about?" She changed positions and leaned forward, resting her chin on her hands.

"Stairs."

"Um, stairs?" She laughed.

I sighed. "Yes. Stairs. Lots and lots of stairs."

"Do they . . . bite?"

"No. They don't bite. But they also don't end. Ever. I've run up and down them for years, and until lately, it's never changed."

She perked up. "It's changed? How?"

"Someone watches me. And today, I found a door to a room where my dad was."

She shivered. "Girl, that's creepy. You say that no one can interpret your dreams, but you've never tried magic, have you?"

"Well, no. Although I don't know why my dad didn't think of that. Probably so he wouldn't have to explain to my stepmom why I wasn't going to the shrink she chose."

"Ugh. Shrinks. I've been to a few of those. Look, let me see what I can do. My mom might be able to help because of the kind of magic she has."

"Any help would be great. I just don't want to make things worse for my dad." I stood up and pulled the blankets on my bed. Judging by the mess they'd become, I must have been restless in my sleep.

"What do you mean, worse?" Jade stood and stretched her legs.

"I don't want to stop having these dreams until I know Dad is safe. So if that's what your mom will do, I don't want it." I followed her out of the room. "So, did I miss anything?"

"Not really. We just had roll call, and then we were told to come back to our cabins and get ready to make our rooms awesome. My mom should be here soon to help us out with ours." Jade dropped onto the couch next to Katy and Heidi, and I took the other chair.

"Oh, so you *are* alive," Katy said.

"Yeah, I was napping. I never got to ask how your dance class went." I pulled off my robe, finally warm after the rainstorm.

"It went well. There were several people there, but it's the first day. Tomorrow they'll probably go to all the magic classes." She picked up a magazine and flipped through it.

"They'd be crazy to skip your classes." Heidi turned to me. "Stretching helps get rid of some of the pain from doing magic. That's why it's included here, along with the other sports. The more in shape you are, the less magic will strain your body."

"That's really cool. Except I still hurt after working out at the batting cages with my dad."

"Oh, you'll still hurt. It just won't be as bad. Come on—I'll show you." Katy slid onto the floor and waited for me. She ran through a couple of different stretches with me, ignoring the knock at the door.

Jade ran to the door and opened it. "Hey, Mom. We're ready for you."

Jade's mom, Sheri, walked into the cabin. "Ah, I see

you're getting all stretched. Perfect. That will make my job easier. We'll start with Katy's room and go from there. Come, girls." Her matter-of-fact manner was different from Jade's easygoing attitude.

I pulled myself up off the floor and followed the girls into the hallway. Jade's mom and Katy stood in the middle of Katy's room.

"Okay, let's get started. I know Katy is ready for this, but we're going to run through it for Sydney's sake. You empty your mind and envision exactly what you want your room to look like. Take a deep breath and then push those thoughts out into the room around you. If it's not right the first time, it's okay. We can try again."

Sheri stepped out of the room and we followed. Katy got into place, closed her eyes, and while she concentrated, I could feel a tingle in the air. I enjoyed the sense of the magic flowing around me without having to deal with the pain afterward. We all gasped as the room suddenly became a small version of a dance studio. A barre ran along one wall in front of a mirror. Her bed was covered in soft blankets and pillows. Pink curtains covered the windows, and a large stereo sat in the corner playing music from *The Nutcracker*.

Katy jumped onto her bed. "Ah, that's nice."

"Okay, while Katy enjoys her new room, we'll move on to Liz's." We followed Sheri into the next room, and Liz stepped forward.

She stood in the middle and closed her eyes. The flash of magic was quick and then her room became an art studio. She grinned and ran over to the canvas and easel. "Perfect!"

Ashley's room was filled with sports memorabilia and beads for crafting. Jade's room was themed with posters covered in peace signs and her quilt was tie-dyed, which I already knew would happen. Heidi's room was filled with fluffy pink pillows and curtains. She flopped on her bed and pulled out a magazine to read.

Then it was my turn, and my stomach bubbled with nervousness. They'd all done this before. My breath caught when I saw everyone coming down the hallway to watch.

"Um, are you girls sure you don't want to enjoy your rooms?" I walked inside slowly, cringing. None of them had shown any pain at all. I hoped it would be the same for me. I shook out my hands and stretched my neck, hoping to calm myself down.

"This is your first time. We like to make sure you have a cheering squad." Jade leaned against the doorway.

"Okay, Sydney. You've watched this five times now. You can do it. Relax, breathe, and then picture what you want." Sheri smiled and backed up.

"Easy for you to say," I muttered. I worked on the meditation Dad had taught me and tried to calm the jitters. I shouldn't have thought of Dad. Pictures of the stairs came to mind and I forced them to go away. I clenched my fists and shook my hands out again. Light, butterflies, rainbows.

I could feel my pulse slow and I relaxed. Okay, castle. Big bed, lots of pillows, sitting room. Breeze coming in through the window. I smiled and pushed the vision out of myself. And my eyes flew open at the gasps from the other girls.

I hadn't tried to think of the stairs just before I pushed. They'd slipped in at the last second, and now they were here. Not the stairs themselves, but the stone walls. Dark curtains covered the windows, and torches surrounded the room instead of the light on the ceiling. My heart beat wildly as I looked over at the doorway.

"Wow, Syd. I never took you for the Gothic type," Katy remarked. The other girls stared at the room from behind her.

"I'm not. This is what I see every night." The terror from my dreams made my bones hurt, but I realized I had no actual pain from the magic.

"Well, unless you want to sleep in this . . . whatever it is, let's try again. Think you can get the right picture this time?" Sheri asked, studying the room.

"Yeah. I had the picture—I just got distracted. I'll try again." I closed my eyes and concentrated on a castle. Not just the room, but the whole castle. I pictured the chandeliers, and the tapestries, and the thick rugs. I pictured the throne room and the main hall, and then jumped to the bedrooms. My room was breathtaking. The deep purples accented the marbled walls perfectly. When I felt certain I could make this happen, I pushed hard.

The "ooh"s and "ahh"s let me know I'd done what I wanted just before I collapsed from searing pain that shot through my body. I tried to keep the scream inside, but it ripped out of me. Shrieks erupted, and I was picked up by several hands and set on top of a bed that was much softer than the one I'd napped on just an hour before.

"Sydney, honey, can you open your eyes?" Sheri's voice was close to my ear.

My eyes didn't want to open, but I finally forced one to obey. I groaned, trying to roll over. Bad idea. Every muscle screamed at me for using my magic.

"You scared us, Syd. What happened?" Liz's voice came from behind me. Wait, I was on my bed. How was she behind me?

I forced my eyes to focus. The bed I'd created was massive. This was not the small room I'd been assigned—I'd made the entire room I'd pictured. "How . . .?"

"You didn't tell me you had that much power." Jade studied the room. "It's almost like we're really in a castle."

I sat up and looked around. "Whoa. I did this?"

Sheri smiled and nodded. "I've never seen anything like it. Cabin eight is not going to like the fact that you took part of their yard."

"I'm sorry. I just did what you told me." I held my head, trying to will away the headache that threatened to knock me back out again.

"You did nothing wrong—I'm highly impressed. It's no wonder you were overtaken by pain. I've never seen so much power used at once." She stood. "I'd better move on to the next cabin. Are you sure you're okay?"

"I just need to sleep." I lay back down and closed my eyes.

"Come, girls. We need to let her rest. We'll see you at the flag ceremony in the morning, Sydney."

I waved and rolled over. I didn't want to sleep for fear of dreams, but the softness of the bed and the warmth of the covers were just too comfortable to leave.

Chapter Nine

When the alarm rang the next morning, I nearly jumped out of my bed, ready to stop this person who had my dad. The stairs had been like a vague memory as they stayed in the background of other strange dreams. I felt more rested than I had in a while, which meant I had more energy to fight.

I stepped onto a thick, soft rug and walked over to the wardrobe that had taken the place of my closet, pulled out my shorts and T-shirt, and quickly dressed. I could hear the other girls talking out in the hallway, so I grabbed my sneakers and opened the door.

"Oh, you're awake. Are you feeling any better?" Jade asked.

"Much. I'm starving, though." I sat down to put my sneakers on.

"Well, let's get to breakfast, then." Katy opened the door.

"Race you!" Heidi called and took off running for the lodge. I chased after her, enjoying the cool breeze.

We reached the cabin laughing and out of breath. Liz had easily won with her long legs, and poor Heidi ended up in last place. She didn't seem to mind as she bounced past us and went straight for the food line.

The smells from the kitchen had my stomach growling. I asked for extras of everything the cooks had to offer, and my plate was piled high with bacon, eggs, sausage, hash browns, and pancakes by the time I sat next to the girls.

"Wow, you weren't kidding when you said you were hungry." Ashley laughed. "Are you going to be able to eat it all?" She took a bite of her pancakes.

"I guess we'll see." I grinned and dug in. The flavors burst in my mouth—everything was cooked to perfection.

I was halfway through when Luke came up to the table with his tray. "Can I sit here?"

Katy jumped up. "You can have my spot. I'm done." She winked at me before taking her plate to the kitchen.

Luke sat down next to me. "How are you feeling today?"

"I'm good." I picked at the rest of my food, suddenly losing my appetite. I was too nervous to eat in front of him.

"I saw your cabin. What happened to it?" He took a bite of his eggs.

"My magic was a little more powerful than I thought. I now have a huge bedroom." I'd been somewhat joking when I'd told Jade I wanted a castle. Who knew I'd actually get it?

"That was you?" he asked, surprised. "That's only happened once or twice before, and never by someone on their first try."

I shrugged. "I didn't mean to. I just pictured the room and pushed, like everyone else. It felt so real, too." Like I'd been there before. Otherwise, how would I have pictured it so perfectly?

"What do you mean?"

"I don't know. The place I pictured is exactly what showed up. I guess it's not what I expected. I figured it would just be a room with a few elements from what we pictured in our minds." I caught Jade and Luke exchanging glances. "What?"

Luke took a drink and cleared his throat before answering. "That's what usually happens. Yours was the exception to the rule."

"You said it's happened before, though." I thought of Katy's ballet room. She'd been happy with what she got, but had she imagined something bigger? Mine was exactly right, down to the last detail.

"It has, but the counselors usually have to step in

and repair the cabin because of severe damage. Your room was intact," Liz said. "You're going to have to teach me how to do that. I'd like a bigger art studio."

"Hey, you won't be changing anything. I don't want you messing up *my* room." Ashley tossed a small piece of toast at her.

"I wouldn't do it this year. I was thinking more for next year. I'll have to try for an end room."

"Excuse me. I need everyone's attention." Sheri stood at the podium at the front of the cabin.

We all turned to listen. Camp was finally getting started, and I felt the excitement build. I wanted to find a way to save my dad, and I was hoping someone here would be able to help me.

"You all should have met your counselors last night. They're the leaders you will turn to with any questions. If you're sick, go to them instead of just skipping class. We need to know where everyone is at all times. Some classes, you'll be taking with your roommates, and other times, you'll have a choice of where you want to go.

"When swimming, please pay attention and watch out for our guests. The mermaids are here for instruction, and we need to respect their territory. Only go swimming during designated times.

"Don't forget that at the end of camp, we will be having a competition against the camp on the other side of the lake. You are encouraged to participate, but if you don't, you are still required to attend.

"You are expected at your first classes in ten minutes. If you don't have a schedule, find your counselor. Now, everyone, have fun, and please obey the rules so we can all stay safe." She sat down and talked to the other counselors.

"Let me guess—you don't have your schedule with you," Jade whispered. "Let's go get one from my mom."

"Meet you at lunch?" Luke asked.

"That would be great." I leaned toward him. "I need to talk to you about something. See you later." I stood and walked with Jade to get my schedule.

We compared our classes and found that we would be going to arts and crafts, followed by working with inanimate objects. We walked together to the arts cabin and waved at Liz before finding a spot to sit. The cabin was full of easels, canvases, and large bins of clay. It had an earthy smell mixed with the strong scent of oil paint.

Each of us had a pottery wheel and clay sitting in front of us. We talked for a bit until the art teacher came in. She was dressed in coveralls and had clay smeared on her cheeks. Liz sat up straighter, excitement showing on her face.

"Welcome, campers. This isn't your typical art class. We'll be doing pottery and a few other crafts, but not in the way you've always learned. You're going to use your magic to work with the clay to make a vase. Instead of touching it directly, you're going to hold out your hands a few inches away and coax it into shape. Watch."

She took the clay in front of her and began to manipulate it into a vase with delicate carvings on the sides. I sat in awe, watching as she worked. "Okay, now your turn. Just concentrate and feel what you want your vase to look like."

I stared at my clay for a minute, unsure what to do. After turning on the wheel, I did what she told us and pictured what I wanted. Putting my hands near the clay, I tried to push my magic into it, but nothing seemed to happen. A glance around the classroom showed me that no one else had figured it out either.

After several minutes, the teacher clapped, and we stopped working to listen.

"How many of you were able to do it?"

Only a couple of hands went up in the air.

"This was to illustrate a point. We can do great things with magic, but we have to know what we want to do with it first. This time, I'm going to teach you how to use the pottery wheel the right way. Next class, we'll try it with magic. Ready?"

We watched as she demonstrated again how to make a vase using her hands with no magic. Once we got the idea, we tried to do it ourselves. This time, I was actually able to make a fairly good-looking vase before the end of the class. I set it aside and washed my hands before leaving with Jade and Liz.

"So, were you two able to do it?" Liz asked.

I shook my head. "This felt different from the magic I used to make my room."

"It is. There are a few different elements. Usually, we're stronger in one than we are in another," Jade explained.

"Except . . ." I thought for a second. "Wouldn't these be the same thing? Both are used to create, right?"

"Yes, but your room was on a big scale. This is on a smaller scale. Think about what kind of magic you've done before. What do you use it for?"

"Well, there was my room. I made myself a pretty awesome dress the other day. And I used it to unlock the car door, so that's small."

Liz looked at me, eyebrows scrunched together. "You unlock your car door with magic? Why?"

"Long story. I'd rather not do it because it hurts." My wrist bones ached just thinking about it.

"So, take Liz here," Jade said. "She does things with her hands all the time. The clay was easy for her because it's just small details. I love things that flow because I can work with wind or water better. Katy uses movement as well, but on a smaller scale. Heidi has a little of everything, as does Ashley."

"I guess that makes sense." I looked at my watch. "We'd better get going."

The class on magic and inanimate objects was a lot of fun as we learned how to change a rock to a marshmallow. A few of the campers popped the marshmallows in their mouths, but I couldn't bring myself to eat it. I was aching all over by the end of the class, but I was happy with how easy the spell had been for me. They rang the bell, and I handed off my marshmallow to Jade.

"Where are you going next?" Liz asked as she walked with me out of the cabin.

"Intro to magic. You?" I put my class paper into my bag.

"I have another art class."

Jade glanced at her schedule. "I have archery. See you later." Jade and Liz waved as I went the other direction.

I walked into the lodge and instantly went on alert. The hairs on my neck stood on end, and my stomach lurched in fear. Someone was here. I whipped around, trying to figure out where they were, but nothing looked suspicious. It didn't make sense with what the woman on the stairs had told me. Why would someone be following me if I was just supposed to pay off a curse?

I left the cabin, hoping I would leave the feeling behind, but it only grew stronger. I needed to hide. I ran back to my own cabin and slammed the door, locking it behind me. I hoped the other girls had their keys. I ran to my room and locked that door as well.

Taking deep breaths to calm down helped a little,

but I could still feel the threat nearby—even though it had lessened significantly. This was no help. I pulled out my cell phone and looked through the list of contacts Dad had programmed into it.

I silently thanked him when I found Luke's number. "Hello? Luke? I need your help."

"Where are you?" His voice came in clearly.

"My cabin. Just hurry, please." My heart beat rapidly. I thought I was safe, that they wouldn't be able to find me here.

"Okay. I'll be right there."

I flipped the phone closed and left my room, watching carefully as I walked into the hallway. Ashley had left her door open and I caught sight of a baseball bat just inside. I grabbed it, figuring it would make a good weapon—if only I could actually see the enemy.

The knock at the door was loud and made me jump. I peeked out the window to find Luke standing on the porch. I set down the bat, unlocked the door, and threw it open.

"What's going on?" he asked.

I grabbed his arm and pulled him away from the cabins. When I felt like we were a safe distance away, I stopped.

"There's someone or something here. Something I feel in my dreams. I can't find it, but I feel it." I shivered.

Luke stiffened. "Where did you first feel it?" He pulled out his phone and started texting.

"I went to my class in the lodge. It was so strong, I ran to my cabin to see if I could escape it, but I felt it there too. It's almost like it's a part of me." Maybe it was—it would explain why the feeling followed me. But again, why?

Luke checked his phone. "Okay, my dad said I'm supposed to stick with you for a bit. Please don't tell me you have something like ballet today."

I laughed. "That would require grace, something I don't have. I'm missing the intro to magic class."

He tilted his head to the side. "Why were you taking that? From what I've heard and seen, you already have pretty good control of your magic." He gestured toward my cabin, now expanded and standing much closer to the one next to it.

"I wouldn't say 'control.' I didn't mean to do that—it just happened. I wanted a small version of a castle room."

"So you have a very vivid imagination. That's a good thing. You'll need it to come up with ways to fight when you're in battle." He waved at some campers who walked past.

I laughed in disbelief. "What battles am I supposed to fighting? I'm at camp. Unless you have a way of defeating an evil stepmom and stepsisters, I'm not sure how learning to battle will help."

Luke grinned. "There's something for everything. That's the joy of magic."

"Perfect. I'd love to turn Sarah into a toad, and Kaylee into a mouse. I'll have to figure out something more fun for Julie." I rubbed my hands together.

"Wow, you're downright evil." He turned and started walking. "Okay, learning to battle with magic it is."

I hurried to catch up. "No way. They don't really have that class, do they?" I was still nervous from the feelings of being watched, but that only made me want to learn to fight even more. I had to protect myself. Mom was gone, and Dad was in a deep sleep.

"No, they don't. But I can teach you. We just have to find an area of the field that's not being used for classes."

"And they won't care that you're teaching me?" I bit my lip. I really didn't want to get in trouble.

"They have archery and sword fighting. They can't really get mad at us for using our magic." He went inside the main lodge and found one of the leaders. I held back, but Luke put his arm around me and pulled me closer. "Hey, Miss Smith. I'm going to be teaching her how to battle. Are you okay with that?" He smiled, his dimples showing. My knees went weak, and I could tell it had the same effect on everyone around me.

Except the counselor. She studied me. "To my office. Now." She turned and walked toward a room at the back of the lodge. She sat in a large, plush chair, and

I sank onto the hard seat across from her. Luke stood behind me, his hands on my shoulders. The warmth from his fingers comforted me.

"Now, would you like to tell me why you want to try to blow up my camp?"

"We don't want—" I burst out.

Luke's hands tightened on my shoulders. "I assume you received notice about her from her father?"

"Yes, I did. And it's all the more reason to keep her magic hidden."

I looked up at Luke, confused. "What does she mean?" I could see his jaw clench.

"It means, Sydney, that until you get your magic completely under control, you are a danger to those around you."

I sat back in shock. "What do you mean? I always have control of my magic. Um, mostly." That wasn't at all what I'd just told Luke, but she didn't have to know that.

She smirked. "Would you like to tell me about your cabin? Did you have that under control?"

"Well . . . no." I should have known she'd hear about that. "But I was able to do things at home all the time without a problem. This time, I just concentrated harder, and it kinda burst out of me." Okay, so that probably didn't help my case. But it really was something I'd never experienced before. Pain, yes, but not letting the magic escape.

"I assume you've only done small things. Opening yourself up to your full potential is completely different. Sheri told me you passed out."

"I guess so. But I was hit with pain so hard and fast, I couldn't take it. I don't think anyone could have," I burst out. I stopped in shock. What was I doing? I never argued with teachers. "I'm sorry. I just . . . want to know why I have so much pain when everyone else seems fine."

Miss Smith paused before speaking. "Do you always hurt that badly when you use magic?"

"I have pain, but it's usually more focused in my arms. I used it to make my dress nicer the other day, and that pain was pretty bad. When I made the first bedroom, I had no pain. The second time, I felt like I was being electrocuted."

"Interesting. We must get that under control." She glanced at Luke. "I will allow you to teach her the basics. But one wrong move—one accident—and you stop. No battling until she has control over her magic. Do you understand?" I hunched down in my chair.

"I understand perfectly. I'll make sure she's careful," he promised.

I stood. "Thank you. I'll do my best."

"I know you will." She left her desk and followed behind us. "By the way, I'm highly impressed with your cabin. There was some pretty amazing detail in your room."

I turned to her in surprise. "You've seen it?"

"During inspections today. There have been some good designs, but never a full suite." She waved and walked over to the other counselors who were talking quietly at the head table.

Chapter Ten

R eady to go?" Luke asked.

"Sure." But I wasn't. I knew practicing magic would hurt, and I didn't want to pass out again. I thought back to the conversation we'd just had.

Luke stopped and faced me. "Syd, look at me."

I met his eyes and got lost in them. "Yeah?" I blinked, trying to pay attention. His blue eyes were way too distracting. At least his dimples were hidden in his concerned expression.

"Things will be okay. We'll get your dad back. And we'll get your magic under control."

"Thanks." I wiped a tear away that suddenly escaped at the mention of my dad. I ached, knowing he was in trouble.

"Any time. Okay, it looks like we have space over there." Luke pointed to a spot on the far side of the archery targets. He marked out a few paces and then faced me. "Now, follow me."

He did a few sweeping motions with his arm before flicking his fingers at his other palm. A burst of fire turned into a small fireball on his hand.

I gasped, amazed at the control he had over the flame. "That was so awesome! Okay, here I go." I copied what he'd done and flicked my hand. The flame roared up before turning into a ball of fire that was twice the size of Luke's. I grimaced at the pain of the magic, but held the ball of fire in place.

His eyes widened. "How did you do that?"

"What? I did the same thing you did." I gestured toward the fireball. "So, um, how do I put it out?"

"Oh! Right." He clamped his hands together, putting out the flame.

"Won't that burn me?" I asked.

"You're the boss. Just decide it won't."

Easy for him to say. I imagined the fire going out and repeated the actions Luke made. Then I laughed when I put out the fire—it hadn't hurt at all.

"Well, I see you have fire mastered." He shook his head. "Let's try water." He pointed at the lake and gestured, almost coaxing it out of its banks. The water rose in a small spout before he pushed his hand down, and the water fell with a splash. "Now you try."

"Do I have to say anything in my mind?"

"Nope. Just coax it."

"Okay." I held my hand out like Luke had and asked the water to go up, but it didn't listen. I tried again, with the same result. I narrowed my eyes and pushed it this time, not giving it a choice.

A huge funnel of water shot up in the air—taking three mermaids with it. Their silvery blue fins sparkled in the sunlight, and their long, flowing hair billowed out around them. Their faces showed surprise at first, followed quickly by anger. I yelped, pushed the water back into the lake, and ran toward it, then leaned over the edge. "Sorry! I'm so sorry!"

One of the mermaids came to the surface. Her mossy green skin enhanced her beauty. "Please be more careful next time. You do not want to mess with us." She glared and swam away, splashing me with water.

"I said I was sorry," I mumbled, wiping off my face.

"Well done, but we'll stay away from the lake, too. I suggest you don't, um, go swimming during camp." He led me away, looking over his shoulder.

"They wouldn't really do anything to me, would they?" I tried to turn, but Luke pulled me farther away.

"Don't look back. They're making some rather impolite gestures, and you don't want to see. Let's get as far away as possible before Miss Smith finds out."

"But it was an accident," I protested. It wasn't like I'd hurt any of them. I wanted to go back and talk to them, but Luke was probably right.

"Yes, the kind of accident she was trying to avoid." We went to the far end of the field, and he thought for moment before dropping his arms to his sides. "Okay, something smaller. But first, how did you feel after that last spell?"

"I . . ." I hadn't felt anything. My jaw dropped. "I'm fine. No pain at all."

He smiled. "You'll feel it later. You pushed the pain away when you forced your power onto the water, but it will come back. It always does. Just pray it's after you're in bed tonight."

"Uh . . . okay. So is that why I didn't see the other girls react to using their magic last night?" That made so much more sense.

"Yep, although you still seem to feel the pain more than most. I think it's because of your unfiltered magic. We just have to learn to filter it. I think you're figuring it out, though. You have to remind the pain to wait until later."

I raised an eyebrow. "Easier said than done?"

"Yes." He laughed. "Okay, I'd teach you to work with wind, but we'd probably have a tornado on our hands. Just know that you'd use that magic the same way you use water. Just coax it where you want it to go.

"So let's do earth. Instead of pulling it up, we're going to dig a hole. This time, concentrate on keeping it small. Tell it what to do, but make sure you keep it under control and only send a little at a time. Again, easier said than done."

He demonstrated by holding his hand out and pushing down, making a twisting motion. A hole began to form, the dirt flying out around it. He stopped and shook his hand, wincing in pain. "Sorry, earth and I don't always agree. I have to push a little harder with this one. Your turn."

I pushed, this time trying to keep it small. The dirt fought back and didn't to do anything. I opened my magic to full power, and soon my hole was twice as deep and wide as Luke's. This time, the pain hit hard, and I doubled over.

Luke put his arms around me, helping me to the ground. "Easy, Syd. You did just fine." He brushed my hair away from my face until I stopped shaking. My body was still screaming at me, but I was able to sit up.

"I can see what you mean about fighting the earth. It fought against me, so I had to push harder. Man, I need a nap." I yawned and covered my face with my hands.

"You've been working hard." He chuckled, staring at the holes we'd just dug. "You really know how to hurt a guy's ego."

"What do you mean?" I was suddenly aware of how close he was and blushed.

"Everything I did, you did twice as much."

"Yes, but I didn't try to. Do you think you'll be able

to teach me better control?" I asked. The thought of going up against someone without knowing how much power I had scared me. I didn't want to blow up the battlefield.

"Of course. Sit by me." He waited for me to position myself so I could watch him. "Now, ask that blade of grass to grow. Just one." He pointed a finger and slowly raised it as the blade grew.

I bit my lip and did the same thing. I thought I was doing pretty well until Luke cleared his throat. "What?"

He nodded behind me. "The lawn guy isn't going to like us much."

The grass was about a foot tall all around me. "Ugh! But I was just talking to one."

"Stop thinking about everything else. Just think of that one blade. Try again."

I sighed. "Okay." I focused completely on the blade in front of me. It rose and sprouted seeds. "I did it!" I couldn't wait to show Dad everything I'd learned. If he ever woke up.

"Great job. Okay, next. You're going to dig a small hole. Very small. And then seek for the water underground to fill the hole."

I stared at him. "Seriously? How?"

He smiled. "You ask it to come to you."

"All right." I pointed down at the ground and told the dirt to move out of the way. I could almost feel it grumble as the hole went a few inches into the ground. I stopped digging and then searched for the water. There it was. Cold water flowed far below the surface. Once I had its location, I asked it to come to the surface. When it refused, I pulled on it until it filled the hole.

I was rather proud of myself until I noticed that the water kept coming. I panicked and pushed it back down, but the water wouldn't obey. Luke jumped up and put his hand out to help me. By the time we were able to stop it, the field was flooded.

"Let's keep you away from water magic, okay? I don't think it likes you. Or maybe it likes you too much." He pulled me away from the puddles. "Come on—let's go before Miss Smith wonders why her field is now a swamp."

"Good idea." I watched the field clear of other campers—a few of them shot glances toward us as they left.

We went to the lodge and got in line for lunch. I waved at Jade and the other girls before grabbing my plate.

"Hey, I'm going to sit with the guys. You okay with that?" Luke thanked the cook for the food and waited for me to answer.

"Of course. Thanks for the help today." I squashed my disappointment. After all, I couldn't have him with me every second.

"No problem. We'll do more later tonight when you've had a chance to rest." He left and went to sit by the guys we'd played baseball with the day before.

I sat next to Katy and took a bite of my chili, suddenly ravenous. I looked up to see everyone staring at me, smiling. "What?"

"What? You've spent the last two days with the hottest guy in camp. Spill." Katy stabbed her salad and took a bite.

I shrugged. "Not much to tell. He helped me with magic."

"Really? I thought we weren't allowed to practice without a teacher," Liz said.

"We got permission first. He took me over to the field and we worked on a few things."

"Oh, so *you're* the one who flooded the field," Ashley said. "Now we can't play soccer today."

Heidi nudged her. "What makes you think it was her? There are five other classes there."

My face grew hot. "She's right. It was me. Apparently, I don't get along with water, so it does whatever it wants."

Ashley glared. "I'll just have to find something else to do, I guess."

"It's not that big of a deal. Besides, we're having a dance tonight anyway." Heidi grinned and peeked over her shoulder at Blake.

The other girls squealed.

"We're having a dance?" I asked, forcing myself not to look over at Luke. I didn't want to get my hopes up.

"I talked Miss Smith into holding one." Katy waved at someone behind me.

"How'd you do that?" Liz asked.

Katy shrugged. "I don't know. I just figured I'd ask. She seemed distracted by something. Of course, that was about the time someone shot the mermaids up into the air." She glanced at me with an eyebrow raised.

"You're welcome." I grinned and finished my food in silence while the other girls talked about what they would wear. Thanks to Kaylee and Sarah, I'd always missed the high school dances. This would be my first, and it made me sick just thinking about it. I wanted to go, but I had no idea what I would do there. Maybe I could just stay in the cabin and no one would notice.

After lunch, I walked to the music room only to find it empty. Strange—we were supposed to be having a class in just a couple of minutes.

I walked around the large room, my steps echoing in the silence. The instruments that lined the walls were arranged into winds, brass, and strings. I'd played a little violin, but it had been years.

Something crashed in one of the rooms to the side. I jumped, my heart beating rapidly.

"Hello?" I stood totally still and listened for any

more sound. When there was only silence, I crept toward to the door and paused. My mind was screaming at me to leave, but I had to know what was in that room. I sensed movement and spun around only to be grabbed from behind. I screamed and clawed at the strong arm that held me fast.

Chapter Eleven

I was on the stairs again—I was tired of them appearing during the daytime. I couldn't tell if I was all the way in my dream, but the pain in my wrist from being dragged behind the man was definitely real. His strides were long and fast, and I did my best not to trip on the stairs.

"Where are we going?" I asked, gasping for air. I would have thought I'd be in good shape from climbing every night, so maybe we really were here all the way. Most of the time, I could go on forever. My mind wandered to Dad. He was here somewhere. Was he okay?

The person said nothing. He just seemed to run even faster. I tripped on a step and fell, crying out in pain. He reached down and pulled me up, not allowing me to catch my breath or check the big bruise on my leg. Apparently, pain wasn't going to get me out of the dream this time.

We came to a door, and he shoved me through before slamming

it shut. I fell down and caught myself with my arms. I could feel my wrist snap, but I held in my scream of pain.

"Ah, Cinderella. There you are." A beautiful old woman sat on a large chair in front of me. Her graying jet-black hair was slicked into a bun, and her burgundy satin dress flowed down to the floor. Servants stood on each side of her, staring straight ahead.

"It's Sydney." I pushed magic into my arm to heal it. I didn't have my dad's skill, but I didn't want to deal with the break any longer than necessary.

"So that's what they're calling you. No wonder I couldn't find you." The woman's smile gave me chills.

I glared. "I'm here every stinking night. It's kind of hard to miss me." The magic was flowing from the center of my belly button and making its way to my wrist. Beads of sweat formed on my forehead as I tried to keep the magic from exploding down my arm.

She clicked her tongue. "Temper, temper. Really, you must learn to respect your elders. Now, where's my payment?"

I lost control of the magic and my wrist snapped back into place, sending waves of nausea through me. I clutched my wrist to my stomach and breathed deeply, trying not to lose my lunch. "What payment?" I asked once my pain had subsided. I knew what she was talking about, but I hoped to hear more from her. I needed some kind of hint so I could get out of this place. Once Dad was safe.

"Don't play games with me. I have been waiting for years to be paid back for your life, and I want it now." Her eyes flashed.

"Look. From what I understand, Mom already paid you.

Now I'm stuck on these stairs for no reason. I want my nights back." I wanted nothing more than to lie down and sleep off the pain of the magic, but I couldn't.

She watched me, her lips pursed and eyes narrowed. "I told your mother I wanted something that would make me happy. She gave me what I asked for, but it didn't please me as I thought it would. Therefore, the curse remains. Find what it is that I want, and I will let you go free." She waved her hand, and I was back in the music room before I could ask what she wanted.

I growled in frustration. How was I supposed to know what to bring her? The room was now dark and I noticed that a few hours had passed, even though it had only felt like minutes. I left the building to find people shouting my name around the campgrounds. Flashlights lit up the night.

I jogged over to Miss Smith. "Hey, I'm here."

Miss Smith startled. "Where have you been? We've been looking all over for you."

"I . . . was taken. But I'm back now. You can call off the search." I could feel my face burning.

She spoke into a radio, letting everyone know I was with her before turning back to me. "Now, would you like to tell me where you were? What do you mean by 'taken'? Do you need help?" Her hand shook as she placed it on my shoulder.

"It's hard to explain. I'm fine, though. Really."

A group of campers gathered around us as we spoke.

I wanted to sink into the ground in embarrassment. Miss Smith cleared her throat and made an announcement.

"Everything is fine now. We'll get the dance started in a few minutes. Go in to the lodge."

As everyone headed toward the dance, a few people glanced at me as they passed by. Jade ran up and grabbed me in a hug.

"Don't ever do that again! You had us worried sick." She tugged on my arm and pulled me into the room behind her. "Spill. Where were you?"

"Just wait until the music starts, okay? I don't want the whole world to hear about it." I nodded toward a few girls who were staring at me. When they realized they'd been caught, they hurried over to the other side of the room.

She leaned closer. "Did it have something to do with Luke?" she whispered.

"What? No. Why?" I looked around. "Where is he?"

"Looking for you. He's frantic, but I wasn't sure if it was real or just an act."

"He's supposed to be watching out for me. Oh, there he is." I waved at him.

Jade sighed. "Fine. Go be with your guy. But you *will* tell me what happened later." She wandered off toward Peter.

Luke dashed over and grabbed me in a hug. "Where were you? You had me so scared."

"Not now." I glanced around at the others who were watching.

As a slow dance started, Luke pulled me onto the floor.

I had to talk loudly over the music as I explained what had happened with the woman in my dream, and when I got to that part of the story, he checked my wrist. "It's fine. Just sore from how fast it healed." I rotated it to show him.

"You had everyone worried when you didn't show up for roll call. I thought I'd lost you." He caressed my cheek before hugging me to him again.

Whoa. My cheek tingled where he'd touched it. It took a second to catch my breath. "I—I'm still here, but I feel more lost than I was before. How am I supposed to find out what makes her happy when I don't even know who she is?"

"We'll figure it out. At least we know what causes your dreams, right? That's a huge thing. I'll tell my dad in the morning so he can help out."

"Okay. For now, let's dance. I want to forget about it." Not that I could. My head felt ready to explode, with all my thoughts running wild.

"My pleasure." He took my hand and spun me out onto the dance floor.

It was a relief to go outside in the cool breeze after the warmth of the lodge. The dance was shorter than it would have been because everyone had been looking for me, but it was still a success. Luke walked next to me, silent. He took my hand and stopped in front of my cabin.

"Thanks for dancing with me. It was a lot of fun." We had stayed together the whole time, only taking a break to get a drink during the fast songs.

"I enjoyed it. Thanks for putting up with me stepping on your toes once or twice." He chuckled, but then turned serious. "I don't like that they can grab you from the camp." He caressed my cheek again, sending tingles down my skin.

"I don't like it either. I hope they'll leave me alone to find whatever it is that she wants. I don't like going there." I shuddered.

"I don't blame you. We'll figure this out. Just . . . don't go anywhere alone, okay?"

"That's probably a good idea. Maybe Jade will let me go to classes with her." I glanced back at the cabin, where I saw several heads suddenly duck down below the window sill.

Luke burst out laughing. "Your friends aren't too smooth with the spying."

"No, they're not." I shook my head.

"I guess this means good night." He bent over and kissed me lightly on the cheek before walking toward his cabin. I stared after him, frozen to the spot. I could still feel his lips and smell his cologne. Never in a million years would I have thought that I'd find a guy at camp who liked me—especially someone like Luke.

I heard the door open, and it knocked me out of my stupor. Touching my cheek where he'd kissed me, I walked inside, waved absently at the other girls, and flopped on my pillows, wanting to think about everything that had happened that night.

The girls burst through the door and jumped on my giant bed.

"Okay, I want to know everything," Jade demanded. "You have way too many secrets."

Katy nudged her. "Everyone has a right to their secrets. I just want to know about Luke."

I laughed. "There's nothing to tell. We danced, and he walked me home. He watches over me." I couldn't keep the memory of his eyes or his dimples out of my head. Okay, so really, I had a major crush on the guy.

"Nothing to tell? He kissed you!" Heidi squealed. "And you didn't dance with anyone else the entire night. And the way he looked at you? Man, he's got it bad." She pretended to faint.

"Oh, brother." Jade rolled her eyes. "What *I* really

want to know is where you went. You were gone for hours. Last thing we knew, you were headed to music class, and then we suddenly had to organize a search party. Out with it."

I hesitated. What if they didn't believe me? Or worse, what if they *did* believe me and didn't want anything to do with me?

Liz smiled and patted my foot. "It's okay. We can help."

"Remember the room I made before this one?" I waved my hand around. "Well, I go there every night in my dreams. We've tried to figure out why for years. Then a few nights ago, I found out it's a debt I have to pay off. Usually I only visit in my dreams, but this time, someone grabbed me and took me there while I was awake. I met this creepy old woman who told me that I had to make her happy in order to break the curse." I ran my fingers through my hair. "Thing is, she sent me back before I could ask her what she wants."

The room was silent for a moment. I knew it—I knew I shouldn't have said anything. I picked at the comforter on my bed, wishing I could climb under the covers and hide away from the other girls. Of course, that would mean going back to those stairs once I fell asleep.

"Wow, Syd. I had no idea. When you said you went there every night, I was thinking like, a recurring dream." Jade leaned over and gave me a hug. "So, are you locked in a room?"

"No. I run stairs. Up or down—it doesn't matter. It's always the same."

"Don't you ever just stop and sit down?" Heidi asked.

"Not really, but I might just do it tonight. I'm tired." I yawned, thinking of how nice it would be to sit instead of climbing. Except . . . "But sometimes I feel like someone's there, watching me, and I've actually felt it a few times while I've been here at camp."

Liz shuddered. "That's creepy." She paused and then brightened. "Maybe she wants a puppy."

"Doesn't sound like it. Maybe you should clean her tower. From the looks of the creepy room you made, it could use some tidying." Ashley shuddered. "I don't know how you stand it."

"I already do enough cleaning at home. I don't want to do it in my dreams too." I rubbed my eyes. "I hate to kick you all out, but I'm exhausted."

Jade climbed off the bed. "Take care of yourself. Night, Syd."

"Have a good night." I waved as Katy closed the door, and then climbed under my covers. As I relaxed, I was hit by a wave of exhaustion and pain that dwarfed anything I'd felt before in my life. It felt as though fire was shooting through my veins. Every bone ached like they were going to shatter. The side effects of the magic I'd used earlier that day finally showed, and I didn't know if I'd survive it.

Trying to get my mind off the agony, I decided to figure out how to make the woman happy. The puppy and cleaning were a long shot. I thought about what I'd seen while I was there, but nothing gave me any clues. She just sat there, all snooty in her chair and fancy gown. Wait—the gown. Maybe I could make a dress she would like. If that's what it took, I'd make her a whole new wardrobe. I knew how to do it, and I was already in pain, so it couldn't get much worse, right? With a plan in mind, I allowed myself to drift off.

Chapter Twelve

Back so soon?" the woman asked.

"Not that I had much choice." I stood in the center of the room, facing her chair again. This time, her dress was a green satin accented by a necklace and earrings encrusted with emeralds. I just hoped this would work.

"No, you really didn't. What did you bring me?"

"I was going to bring you a gown."

The woman studied me for a moment. "As you can see, I already have gowns. Why are yours so much better?"

"I make them using magic." I held my hands behind my back to hide their shaking.

"What—you're going to crochet me a dress or something?" The woman's laugh was like ice down my back.

"No. Do you have an old dress lying around?" I asked. This would only work if I had something to start with.

The woman waved her servant away, and he brought back an old tattered gown.

"Okay, watch." I closed my eyes and imagined a rich maroon dress with ribbon around the neck and sleeves. I threw in some embroidery just to see how it would work, and then pushed it toward the dress in front of me.

The woman gasped. "How did you do that?"

I opened my eyes, a wave of exhaustion nearly knocking me off my feet. "I just told the dress what to look like."

The woman stood and came toward me. She took the dress and inspected it closely. "This is perfection." She glanced over at me. "I have never seen its equal."

I was proud of what I'd done. I shook out my hands, trying to rid them of the pain from the magic. It felt different here. Easier to use. "Does this mean I'm done? Did I break the curse?"

She looked at me in surprise. "Of course not. This is beautiful, but it is not what I wanted. Come back and try again." She flicked her hand, and the dream faded out.

The next morning came way sooner than I wanted. My muscles screamed as I stretched. After the pain I'd dealt with the night before, it wasn't surprising that my body didn't want to behave. I stood and touched my toes and did a few other exercises until I was loose enough to move without wanting to cry.

I changed into a T-shirt and shorts and hurried out of the cabin. I was starving and didn't want to wait any longer for breakfast. My legs didn't want to move fast, so I had plenty of time to enjoy the scenery. The sun reflected off the lake and sparkled, reminding me of diamonds. I stopped walking and watched the water. What if I could make my own? Every girl liked jewelry, right? The dress hadn't satisfied the woman, but I bet jewels would. I'd have to ask the art teacher for help after breakfast.

I finished up the last of my pancakes and waved goodbye to my friends. The wind had picked up while I was eating, and I had to pull my hair up into a ponytail to keep it out of my face.

The door to the art cabin was locked when I tried to go in. I was disappointed, but it made sense—the counselors and teachers would need to eat as well. I sat on the top step and watched as campers walked by to their different classes. The trees moved in the breeze, and the lakes had small waves on the surface. After several minutes, I saw a woman heading for the cabin.

"Can I help you?" the camp leader asked. Her name tag read "Anne" in bold letters.

"I'm just anxious to learn." I smiled.

"Well, come on in. You can help me get things set up." She unlocked the cabin, headed past all the desks and easels, and opened the art closet. "Take these and put one on each desk, please."

"Okay." I took the bottles of paint from her and passed them out. I couldn't bring myself to make small talk, so I just kept quiet until she spoke to me.

"Were you in this class yesterday?" she asked.

"Um, no. I was in pottery. And I'll go there later. I just . . . had a question." Now that I was here, I was too embarrassed to ask.

Anne looked up from what she was doing and wiped her hands. "What is it?"

"Well, it's dumb. I just wondered if there was a way to make jewels or something with magic. But now, never mind. I'd better get to my class."

"Wait. It's Sydney, right?"

"Yes." I blushed. Everyone probably knew my name by this point.

"Why are you asking how to make jewels?" She studied my face closely.

I couldn't figure out any other reason, so I figured I'd tell some of the truth. "I just wondered … it's for payment." I backed toward the door. This was a mistake.

"Payment for whom?"

"A lady. But just forget it. I'll figure out something else." I turned to go.

"Are you in trouble?"

"No. Well, kind of. She has my dad." My stomach turned, thinking of him lying there. I took a deep breath, trying not to cry.

"She has your dad? Have you called the police?" Anne hurried forward and put her hands on my shoulders.

"No. The police can't help him where he is. I'm supposed to find what makes her happy. I just figured that jewels would make anyone happy. But it was dumb."

Anne glanced behind me. "There are other campers coming to class. Come back during lunch. I can help you, but you really should report this to someone."

"I've told you and Luke, but there's nowhere else to go. He's going to contact his dad today and let him know what's going on. They should send help. But I think this is something I need to do on my own. I'm not sure she'd bend for anyone else." I opened the door. "I'll be back at lunch. Thank you." I smiled and hurried out of the way of the other campers.

I slipped into my chair in pottery class and listened closely as the counselor taught us how to use magic. This time, I was able to make my clay resemble a vase. I wouldn't be doing it for a living anytime soon, but it was still a vase.

My next class was a lot of fun, and I came up with a way to make a chair walk. Maybe I could use that on a footstool so the woman could be more comfortable.

Luke caught up to me on the way to my next class. "Hey, ready for another lesson?"

It sounded better than the class I was supposed to

attend, and I'd already missed the first session yesterday for lessons with Luke. "Sure. Where should we go?"

"Let's avoid the field. I think the mermaids complained to Miss Smith." He grinned and put his arm around me as we walked.

"The lodge is full. We could use my cabin, maybe."

"Boys aren't allowed in the girls' cabins." He was silent for a moment. "Do you trust the forest?"

I glanced over at it. "I don't know. I guess it's better than nothing, but there was that cloaked person out there our first day here. We never did figure out who it was."

"I'll take him down if he shows up again. Or you will. That's what we'll be working on today." He led me out to the forest, and we walked for a bit until we came to a clearing.

"At least the mermaids are safe, but I'm not sure about the animals." I watched a squirrel scamper off.

"They'll be fine. Now, we're going to be learning how to put up shields so you're not hit with any spells your enemies cast."

"They don't usually throw anything at me—I just end up there in my dreams. But yesterday, he grabbed me from behind." I couldn't help glancing over my shoulder to make sure no one was there.

"That's not very sportsmanlike. Okay, we'll learn self-defense after this, then. You're going to take the force you used to control the wind and imagine a large shield in front of you. Then push it toward the attacker. You try."

"Whatever you say, sir." I held up my hands and tried to picture a shield. When I thought I had it down, I pushed it at Luke. A rush of air flew from my hands and hit Luke head-on. He flew backwards onto the ground, landing hard. I ran over to him, panicked. "I'm so sorry. Are you okay?"

Luke rolled over, gasping for air. "I've been better. Let's have you try it on something else." He stood, groaning. "Man, you pack a punch."

"I didn't mean to. I just did what you said." I helped pull the leaves out of his hair before backing away. "Okay, so I won't use this against you. How should I practice instead?"

"Use that tree over there. It looks sturdy enough." He rubbed the back of his head. "Do the same thing, but this time, try to control how much magic you use."

I nodded. "Okay." I concentrated on the shield, and this time, I didn't push quite as hard. The tree still rocked as it was hit with the shield, and leaves fell as the branches whipped around.

"I think that would stop an army. Try one more time, and think of it more like a flick of the wrist instead of a full-on push."

"All right." I tried again. This time, the branches only moved slightly.

"Perfect. Now, one more time with me. I want you to count to three, but be ready to throw the shield because I'm going to throw something else at the same time." He walked several feet away and got into a fighting stance.

My heart beat rapidly as I tried to concentrate on what I was supposed to be doing. "One, two, three!" I threw out the shield and ducked, afraid of what he was going to throw.

I slowly lifted my head, wondering if I'd hurt him again, but he was standing there, hands on his hips.

"What was that?" he asked.

"A shield?" I asked.

He pointed behind me. "Not a very strong one."

I turned. A tree was smoldering, hit by two curses, from the look of the marks on its trunk. I pulled lightly on the water from a nearby puddle and shot it toward the tree, putting out the fire.

"Well done with the water, but we still have to work on your shields. Come on."

We tried several more times until I could push away his curses. He showed me a couple of my own to try, and I had them down after several minutes. The fireball was harder to control, but I loved shooting the flames. The ball of ice came easily, and I had to stop so I wouldn't kill the tree I'd been practicing on.

"Can we move on to self-defense? I think it's almost

time for lunch, and I'm starving. Plus, I'm really tired from all this magic."

"Oh, right. Let's start with a few escapes from the front." He grabbed my wrist with both arms. "Now grasp your fist and pull up as hard as you can."

I tried what he said and yanked my hand out. "Awesome. What's next?"

Luke showed me two more escapes, and I quickly caught on. "Now for the harder ones." He moved behind me and grabbed me by the shoulders. "Use the same pressure points I showed you and slip out."

I tried to concentrate on what he was saying, but I couldn't get over the fact that his arms were around me. My fingers trembled as they reached for the pressure points.

"Syd? Are you okay?" he asked softly.

I gulped. "Yeah, I'm fine." I shoved his hotness factor out of my head and pushed on his pressure points before getting away.

"There you go. Let's try another one." Luke pulled me close, and his breathing next to my ear distracted me again.

I really needed to get this done. *Then* I could drool over him. I went through the steps as he slowly walked me through them. By the time I had it down, I'd convinced myself that he was the bad guy, and I was able to get out quickly.

He rubbed his stomach after I punched him during one of my escapes. "I'd better watch out how I approach you now. I'd hate to surprise you."

"I'm pretty strong. Don't mess with me." I flexed, then laughed as he tackled me to the ground. "Hey, that was totally unfair. I wasn't ready." I pushed him off, giggling, and stood up.

"Yes, well, I'm a ninja, so you never know when to expect me." He laughed. "Now let's go before I starve to death. Race you!" He took off running, and I had to sprint to catch up.

"So what are your plans after lunch?" Luke asked as he picked up a tray for each of us and handed one to me.

"I'm meeting with one of the counselors."

"Okay, I'll see you after that. A couple of the guys want to play some basketball."

"Sounds good. See you then." I picked up the last of my food and carried it over to sit by Jade. "Hey, what's up?"

"Not much. How was your training with Luke?"

"It was fun. He taught me how to fight and some self-defense."

"So is that all you were doing? Or was there kissing involved?" Heidi asked. "Ow!" She glared at Ashley.

"Like that's any of your business," Ashley said. "But was there?" Her eyes danced.

"Nope. Hard to do when I'm throwing fireballs at him." I took a drink of my juice.

Jade stood up with her tray. "I'll see you guys later. I want to watch the basketball game, and the guys just took off."

"See ya." I finished the rest of my lunch and walked over to put my plate away. There was only half an hour left of lunch, and I needed to see what Anne could teach me. The door was open when I got to the art room, and I slipped inside on alert. "Hello?"

"Oh, Sydney. I'll be right there," Anne called from another room.

I walked around the classroom, looking at all the paintings the other campers had done. Some were pretty simple, but others were beautiful with their detail. I was pulled in by one painting of a castle on a hill, strangely feeling like I'd been there before. I reached out to touch it.

"Okay, let's get started."

I startled, not realizing Anne had come into the room. "So, what do we do?"

"Sit down and I'll show you. These aren't anywhere near as valuable as real jewels, but we can make some fakes that look real." She pulled out some different stones and put them inside a box. "These will have to undergo large amounts of heat, so I hope you've learned to control your fire magic."

"Um, mostly. Luke was just teaching me."

"Wonderful. Okay, make a fireball and hold it over

the stone until it changes. Depending on the strength of your magic, it could take minutes or hours. The longer you can hold it, the better it will be. Most wizards don't make their own because it takes so much energy." She looked up at me. "From what I hear, you have more power than you know what to do with. Let's see how it works."

I sat down in front of her and made the fireball before pushing it onto the stones. After several minutes, Anne told me to stop.

"Wow, you really are strong. See these crystals?" She pointed out tiny bits of colored stone lining the rocks I'd been working on. "That's impressive. Keep it going, and I'll be right back."

I nodded, focusing my attention on the stones. I could see them changing in front of my eyes and I didn't want to stop. The woman would *have* to like these, right? I mean, I knew she probably wanted something more valuable, but it couldn't hurt to try.

Anne sat in front of me again and pulled out some other stones. "Okay, you have those mastered. Let's try a diamond. This time, you need pressure more than you need heat. So think . . . heavy." She took the rocks I'd been working on and put other rocks in their place.

I cupped my hands and pushed down as hard as I could, trying to use heat and wind together. I added water to the mix and watched as the rock slowly changed. I suddenly felt an overwhelming surge of exhaustion, so I pushed one more time before having to rest my head on the desk in front of me.

Anne rushed over. "Oh, dear. You worked yourself way too hard. I shouldn't have taught you this." She hurried over to her desk, and I could hear her talking to someone as I faded into blackness.

I woke to a large headache, and I groaned and covered my eyes. My body screamed at me when I tried to move, so I remained still.

I opened my eyes one more time to see that I'd ended up in my room somehow. By the light streaming in my windows, I could tell it was late in the day. Katy, Jade, and the others were sitting nearby, watching me, reading, or painting their nails.

"How long did I sleep?" I managed to ask. I needed water.

Katy rushed over. "You're awake! Man, you had us worried. How are you feeling?"

"Like I want to sleep for years." I groaned. "Can you get me some water?"

Heidi left and came back with a cup. "Here you go."

Jade and Katy helped me up in bed while Heidi held the cup for me.

I caught a flash of light to the side of me and looked over. The stones sat on the table by my bed. One was half transformed into a diamond, and the other had small crystals embedded in it.

"The art teacher sent these with you. She said you made them." Heidi tilted her head to one side. "How did you do that?"

"By pushing myself way too hard." I flopped back on my pillows. "Remind me never to do that again."

"Are they real?" Katy picked one up.

"They're not worth anything, but they're real enough." Ashley picked up the other one. "This is hard magic. Why were you doing it?"

"To break the curse. Can you hand them to me? I have to take them into my dream." I yawned, still drained from working so hard.

Ashley and Katy handed over the rocks and went to the door, followed by the others.

Jade turned. "You be careful. And let's have fewer near-death experiences, okay?"

I smiled, already having a hard time keeping my eyes open. "Got it."

Chapter Thirteen

I t took several flights of stairs and a couple of rest breaks before
I was able to find the woman again. I pushed the door open and
stumbled in.

"Why, Cinderella. I wasn't expecting you for a while."
The woman was dressed in a navy blue velvet gown and held a small
silver goblet. Guards stood on each side of her, staring straight
ahead.

"Stop calling me that. It's Sydney. And I brought you
something." I still ached from making the gems, but I wanted to get
this over with so I could find a place on the stairs to hide and sleep.

"Oh? And what's that?" She gestured for me to come closer.

I walked forward, holding the stones tightly, and prayed she
would at least be impressed. The woman took the jewels from me
and I stepped back, biting my lip.

She studied one stone and then the other. "Where did you get
these?"

"I . . . made them." I'd hoped she wouldn't ask that. She didn't seem above making people use their magic to get what she wanted. After all, I was stuck in these stairs because of her.

Her eyebrows shot up. "You made them? I don't believe it."

My anger flared. "I did. My body back in the real world is exhausted. It took everything I had to make them."

She leaned forward, studying my face. "How?"

"My art teacher taught me to push fire and wind into the stone. I added water to harden it." I caught her hungry expression, and I didn't like it.

"Do it again." Her smile was a little forced, and the way she leaned forward made me back up a few steps.

"No. It almost killed me."

"Do it. If you really have that much power, I want proof." She snapped her fingers, and a short, thin guard hurried to her side. "Get me some rocks. Quickly."

I clenched my hands into fists. This wasn't possible. I barely had control over my magic when I was awake—how was I supposed to control so much of it in my sleep?

The little guard brought back a couple of stones and waited for another man to set up a table.

"I'll melt the table." I looked up at the woman. "I use a huge fireball. This isn't going to work—I can just do it on the floor."

The woman smiled. "The table is fireproof. Now, let's see what you can do." She leaned back, lacing her fingers together.

I took a deep breath before putting my hands over the stones. I hesitated and glanced up at her. "This might not work. I'm tired and I'm not awake."

She brushed away my concern. "You'll do fine. Now, get on with it. No more stalling."

"Fine." I made a ball of fire and pushed down. I was surprised to see that I didn't have to push as hard this time. I stopped and stretched my cramped muscles.

She laughed in delight. "Excellent. I'll have to think on this. For now, I'll give you two nights of rest. Use them wisely." She waved her hand, and the room faded away.

I woke and tried to sit up, but I still couldn't move without pain. I made a mental note that doing magic in my dream may have been easier, but it still had its consequences. Along with the pain came ravenous hunger, so I pulled myself out of bed and limped to the bathroom. After a hot shower, I was ready for the day—mostly.

Jade had stayed back to walk to breakfast with me. "So what happened last night? You were so restless, you woke me up."

"I had to make more jewels for the woman in my dream. She gave me no choice." I could still see her hungry expression when she'd heard what I could do.

"Ugh. You must be exhausted."

"I could sleep for another few days." I saw Anne in the distance, and thought back to the day before. "Hey, how did I get home from the art cabin yesterday?"

"Anne radioed for help, and the counselors carried you back. Luke wouldn't leave your side until you were in bed, and then stayed out on our porch until this morning." She looked over at me, smiling. "He must really like you."

"I guess so." I felt a little lighter as we walked into the lodge. It was nice to have Luke as a protector.

We had to eat breakfast quickly because we were going to be working on our events for the competition.

My roommates headed off for their activities, and I wandered toward the archery field. It was the only thing I felt good about doing, besides baseball. The mermaids were racing across the lake as I walked past. They were fascinating to watch, with their tails flashing out of the water. When I got to the field, there were several other campers practicing. My heart leaped when I noticed that Luke had just gotten there as well.

"Hey, Luke." I zipped up my sweater to block out the cold morning breeze.

"I didn't expect to see you up yet. How are you feeling?" He gave me a hug and handed me a bow.

"I'm sore, but good. The jewels I made were enough to impress her, so she's giving me a couple nights of rest." Not that I believed her. I hadn't had two days off from those stairs since I started having the dreams years before. We stepped aside so other campers could walk past us.

"That's great! Now you can finally get the rest you need, and we can think of other ways to help break the curse."

"Yeah, I can. Or I can ignore her and enjoy my freedom." I grabbed some arrows and followed Luke out to a target. "So, how does this work?"

"Well, you shoot at the target over there."

I giggled. "That's not what I meant. How does the competition work?" I took aim at the target and shot, sinking the arrow near the bull's-eye.

"Nice. You're getting better all the time." He took his turn, hitting the center. "We shoot at twenty-five yards, fifty yards, and then one hundred yards. The lowest three drop out each time."

"Maybe this isn't the best event for me, then." I hadn't shot anything past twenty-five yards, and I was terrible at that. But then, I didn't know how to do anything else but baseball.

"Maybe not, but we need a few more for the event. Besides, this way you can hang out with me, right?"

"True. I suppose I could humiliate myself for that." I shot a few more, hitting the target each time.

Luke stepped close and put his hand over mine. "You need to loosen up. Stop worrying about where it's going to hit it and let it go."

I was distracted by his closeness, but it did the trick. The arrow went straight to the bull's-eye. I jumped up and down and threw my arms around Luke's neck. "I did it!"

He laughed and hugged me back. "I knew you could. Now, let's try it again."

We took turns shooting, and by the time we had to go in for lunch, I'd hit the bull's-eye several more times.

Luke took my hand as we walked to the lodge together, sending a thrill of excitement through me. Once we collected our food, we found a table in the corner and sat.

"So, are we still ignoring everything that happened last night?" Luke popped a French fry in his mouth.

"What are you talking about? I simply went to bed in my room fit for a princess and woke up this morning. Nothing else happened." I smiled innocently.

"Of course. So, tell me about your plans for school."

I picked at my salad. "That's a good question. I want to get into a good college and do something with science, but my grades have been so bad, I don't know what I'll do."

"What happened?" Luke asked. The sympathetic way he looked at me made my heart race.

"The stairs. I can't concentrate most of the time. I've done better over the last few weeks because the dream changed, but before, I could barely survive. Between doing chores for my stepmom and stepsisters and having to deal with these dreams, I don't get any sleep or time to study." I stabbed a carrot and shoved it in my mouth, trying not to cry.

"You do chores for your stepmom and sisters? What do they do all day?"

"They shop. Or find other ways to make me miserable. They've broken most of what used to be my mom's." My thoughts drifted back to my blanket that was still in pieces. I hadn't had a chance to fix it before I left for camp.

"Man, I'm sorry, Syd. That isn't fair. Does your stepmom know about these dreams?"

"Yeah, her way of fixing it was to send me to a psychologist. We stopped telling her about them and she finally dropped it. We keep all magic away from them. Dad didn't feel like they should know, for some reason. I'm fine with that—it's one thing they can't come after me for." I pushed my plate away. The lodge was slowly emptying out, but I didn't want to end our conversation. "Enough about me. What are your plans?"

"I've thought of studying to be a doctor, but I would also like to follow in my dad's steps and help out in the magical world. I'm already starting with it." The excitement in his eyes when he talked about working with his dad made me smile. I knew exactly how he felt.

"That sounds great. I think that even though I want to do something with science, I'm going to do the same thing. I haven't been able to get away because it would look suspicious to my stepmom, but as soon as I'm old enough to leave the house, I want to travel with my dad and see what I can do to help the world. Who knows—maybe I can combine science and magic."

Luke leaned forward. "I bet you could. With the power you have now, you could do pretty much anything you wanted." He shook his head. "I just don't understand how you have so much magic, but you never used it. Did you even know?"

"Nope. I had to be sneaky, so I only got to do small things with it." It hadn't even dawned on me to use my magic for anything more than opening doors. Even making the dress was something out of the ordinary for me.

"That's too bad, because the world could use more of your power." His eyes danced.

"I think the mermaids would disagree with you." I pulled my plate back and took a few more bites. His words warmed my heart. It was nice hearing compliments from anyone, let alone a totally adorable guy.

"Well, that just means you'll have to stay away from them as you become rich and famous. Come on. I hear there's a pickup baseball game after lunch—let's go play. Maybe you can get on the team for the competition."

I jumped up. "Let's go. I can't pass up a game."

We got our mitts from our cabins and then headed

over to the field. Luke and I were put on different teams again, and I went to the dugout so we could bat first.

I groaned when I noticed Nick sitting on the bench, writing down names. He sneered when he saw me come into the box. Thankfully, he turned away instead of saying something to me. The umpire blew his whistle to get the game going, so Nick stood to pick a bat. Of course he'd put himself first on the roster.

Once the pitcher was ready, Nick went out and knocked the first pitch to the fence. He made it to home, and Max was up next. After a few more runs, it was our turn to take the field.

Nick put me in right field, and I ran to get into position. I stood, waiting for a ball to come to me, and felt like something wasn't quite right. The feeling of being watched was back—I was supposed to be left alone. I shook it off and watched as runner after runner hit the ball over to left or center field.

When Luke took his turn at bat, I could have sworn he grinned at me. He hit the ball, and it came flying straight to me. I caught it and threw it in, making it a triple play.

"Wow, Syd, that was awesome!" Max clapped me on the shoulder once we got to the dugout.

"Thanks. You did great getting them out on third." I sat down next to him. I would be up after a few more batters.

"Yes, but if you hadn't caught it, I couldn't have made it work." He watched me pull on some batting gloves. "Do you play in high school?"

"No, but I play in a city league." When my stepmom let me out of the house, which wasn't often. I stood and checked out the available bats. I found the heaviest one that felt good in my hands and went out to practice my swing. Nick slid home, and then it was my turn.

We were tied going into the ninth inning, and by the time we took the field the last time, Nick's face was one giant storm cloud. He got the first two batters out, and then Luke took his turn at bat again. He hit the ball out to left field and sprinted around the bases, making his team ahead by one point. The next batter hit it right to me and the game was over. We ran in to cheer for the other team.

"Your school is crazy not to have you playing for them." Max shook his head in admiration. "That was awesome. Please tell me you're playing at the competition."

"I'm planning on it. Unless someone else has a problem with it." I looked right at Nick, who grumbled something under his breath and walked away. We did our cheer and ran to shake hands with the other team.

I went back to the dugout to grab my gloves. As I left, Nick stood in my way, his arms folded. "Enjoy your couple of nights off. They'll be your last." He laughed cruelly and turned to walk away.

I stood there in shock, watching his back. He was the right size to be the guy in the cloak. And that feeling I got around him . . . I couldn't move. How had I not picked it up before? I'd brushed past him that day at the lodge when I felt like I was being watched. I just hadn't paid attention to him.

"Nice game, Syd—what's wrong?" Luke glanced behind him.

I swallowed, trying to make my mouth work. "He— Luke, I think he's the guy who took me into the dream." My hands were shaking. He had plagued my nightmares for so long, and he had been standing right next to me. My legs were Jell-O.

"Nick? Are you sure? I mean, the guy's a jerk, but how do you know?"

"He told me to enjoy the next couple of nights off. And he's just the right size to be the guy in the cloak." It was no wonder Nick was so rotten to me.

Luke pulled me into a hug, squeezing me to him. "Well, that explains a lot. We have guards around the perimeter of the camp, so we couldn't figure out how he got in. All this time, it was one of the campers."

I nodded. "But how do we stop him?"

"We keep you away from him." He let go, pulling me toward the cabins. "We'll just have to know where he is at all times and stay on the other side of camp. I need to talk to Max and a few other guys."

"Wait—they know about all this?" My stomach plummeted. How many people knew about me?

"No, but they've seen how Nick treats you. We'll just play on that. I can't let him take you again."

"But I'm supposed to have a break. This is ridiculous. Can't I go hide in the pottery room or something?"

"That's actually a great idea. Doesn't Liz like art? Maybe she can stay with you while I call my dad to tell him what's up."

"Yeah, but I don't want her pulled into this." I jogged up the steps of my cabin, but Luke stopped me before I opened the door.

"Sydney, she's part of it just by being in the same cabin. We need to stop Nick, and right now, this is our only option." He caressed my cheek and leaned in to kiss me softly, making my knees weak. All the fear drained away, leaving nothing but joy. He pulled away and cupped my face in his hands. "I can't lose you."

"Okay." I turned away and fumbled with the doorknob. My brain was still buzzing from the kiss, and I paused for a second, trying to remember what I was doing. "Hello? Liz? Anyone?"

Katy came into the living room. "Liz is at her art class. What's up?"

"I just wanted to see if she could go to the pottery room with me." I stepped into the cabin, and Luke leaned up against the doorframe.

"Why can't Lover Boy go with you?" She winked at Luke and dropped onto the couch.

Luke laughed. "I have to make a phone call, or I would. Sydney needs protection, and I figured you girls might be willing to help."

"Protection? What's going on?" Katy hopped up from the couch, her eyes wide.

"I think Nick is the guy who kidnapped me," I explained. I knew it sounded crazy, but there wasn't much I could do about that. It was the story of my life.

"That jerk. Are you sure?" She pulled on her shoes.

"I'm not positive, but he knows things about last night's dream that he shouldn't." I followed her outside as she brushed past us.

"Hey, I'm going to take off. I need to catch Dad before he heads into meetings." Luke kissed me again and jogged toward the entrance to camp.

Katy raised her eyebrow. "So, are you still going to deny that he likes you?"

I couldn't help grinning. "No. It's so weird, though. I don't know why he sticks around." We walked toward the art cabin.

"He likes you. That's all that matters." She pulled a rubber band out of her pocket and put her hair in a ponytail. "So what was it that Nick knew?"

"The woman had me prove I made those gems. When I was able to create more, she gave me a few nights off from running the stairs. Today, Nick told me I should enjoy them because they would be my last." I shuddered.

Katy stopped. "Wait. You made them again? In your sleep?"

I sighed. "I know it sounds weird, but lately I've been dragged into my dreams, and I found out today it's Nick who's been doing it."

"I just don't get how you can go inside your dreams. I thought no one knew how to do that anymore."

I looked at her, stunned. "What do you mean? I didn't know anyone else had ever done it. Well, except the ones torturing me." There were others who could do what I did? Why hadn't Dad said anything about them?

"It used to happen all the time a few centuries back, but it was banned and the magic was lost. It was around the time the cost for magic became pain."

"But that doesn't make sense. I walk in my dreams every single night, but I have more pain than other people when I use magic."

She shrugged. "It affects us all in different ways, I guess." We stopped outside the art building. "What I don't get is how that woman can get Nick to walk in and out of your dreams."

"I don't know, but it's really annoying." I pulled open the door to the art cabin and went inside. Liz sat at the back of the room, making a bowl. A few strands of her red hair had fallen in her face, and she stared intently at the clay in front of her.

"Looks like I'll have to stay with you," Katy whispered. "I'm not sure she'd notice if someone came in and battled you right in front of her. She loves her art." She pulled a chunk of clay from the bin and handed it to me, then grabbed some for herself. "It's like me with dance. It's easy to lose yourself in what you love."

I stared at the clay in my hands. What did I love that much? Sports? I sat by a wheel and tried to make the clay obey my fumbling hands, but it was hopeless. I stared at it, thinking. I pushed and prodded, using my magic, and as I added a little of the different elements, the clay started obeying. I imagined an old vase and started forming the clay into what was in my mind.

When I got the clay to look how I wanted, I stopped the wheel and blew a curl out of my face. I lifted the vase and examined it, happy with my work.

"Wow, Syd, that's pretty amazing. Much better than mine." Katy held up the small flower pot she'd made.

"Hey, it's nice. I like it."

Liz blinked and turned off her wheel. "When did you get here?"

Katy laughed. "About an hour ago."

Liz blushed. "Sorry. I was trying to get this to look right for my mom's birthday next week." She gestured toward the bowl in front of her. It was far beyond anything I could have imagined making.

"It's beautiful. The detail you added around the top

is amazing." I picked up my vase carefully. "Where do we put these?"

"Thank you. There's a drying room in the back." She led us to the room, and we set them out to dry. "I haven't seen you two in here much."

"Syd's hiding. We figured this was the last place Nick would look for her." Katy went to the sink to wash the clay off her hands. "I need to teach my dance class. You're good with Liz now?" She dried her hands and turned to me.

"Yes. Thanks for watching out for me."

Katy waved and ran out of the cabin.

"Why does Nick want you?" Liz asked, pulling out more clay. She set it on her wheel and sat back down.

I told her what was going on. She gasped when I told her what I'd done in my sleep, but she didn't say much else.

"Well, stay with me as long as you want. Dinner should be soon anyway."

"Thanks, Liz." I set my clay on the wheel. "So why do you come here instead of working in your room?"

"I have canvas and paint, but not a potter's wheel. I guess I could make one, but I love the smells in here. Plus, I have to force myself to leave the cabin or I'd stay in there for years." She laughed.

"Right. I understand that." I started working the clay in front of me and had made it into a salad bowl with a few ridges by the time the dinner bell rang.

We put our stuff away and cleaned up around our wheels before heading over to the lodge. I looked at my clay-spattered clothes and wished I'd put on coveralls before working.

"Hey, Syd, how was pottery?" Luke came up to stand in line behind me.

"It was fun. I made a couple of things." I smiled at the cook as she served me lasagna and a piece of garlic toast.

"That's great. Are you going to the campfire tonight?"

"Probably. Unless you think it's a bad idea." I glanced over at Nick, who was absorbed in his dinner.

"Hey, I'm there to protect you this time. Besides, I want to hang out." His smile made my heart melt.

"Sounds good to me. It's much more exciting than sitting in my cabin all night." I followed him over to sit by Liz and my roommates.

Luke squeezed my hand before we started eating, and we talked about the upcoming competition. The warmth and contentment I felt was something I usually only experienced when it was just my dad and me. I hated for camp to end. Tomorrow was the last day to practice—we'd be heading over to the other camp early Friday morning.

Sheri stood at the front of the lodge. "Can I have your attention, please?" She waited for everyone to quiet down.

"We've decided that tonight's campfire will include a talent show. It can be dancing, singing, whatever you'd like. Since Friday's competition is all about sports and outdoorsy things, we decided to let everyone else show off their other skills tonight. Campfire will start in an hour." She sat down to the buzzing of excited voices flowing through the lodge.

"Are you dancing, Katy?" I asked. I would definitely sit this one out. I hadn't taken a violin lesson in years, and singing was not an option.

"Yeah, this is awesome. I get to have my class show their stuff." She smiled and pointed. "Look how many people are leaving to get ready. I'm not the only one excited for this."

Heidi and Ashley hopped up and grabbed their trays, talking in excited whispers.

"Where are you two going?" Katy asked. She took a bite of her salad and waved at a group of her dancers as they walked by.

"We have to practice. We're going to sing," Ashley said and hurried off to dump her plate.

"I didn't even know she sang." Not that I spent much time with them. Luke kind of took up my free time.

"They're both pretty good." Liz said. "They sing together at talent shows back home all the time." She picked at her salad before pushing it away.

"Are you doing anything?" I asked her.

She shook her head. "All my stuff is art. I don't know if anyone would want to watch me paint a picture." She shrugged. "It's okay, though. I might just hang out at the cabin."

"You should come and sit with me. I don't plan on performing either." I smiled at her.

Jade jumped up. "See you guys there. I need to grab my guitar." She met up with Peter and they walked out of the lodge together, hand in hand.

I finished my last bite. "You two ready to go?"

"Yep. I was going to grab seconds, but I think I'll save room for S'mores later." Luke stood, and we followed him out of the lodge.

The campfire was in the middle of the field, with log benches set around for the audience. A stage had been brought in, complete with lights and microphones. The performers signed up as they got to the area. I'd missed last night's campfire because of the whole not-being-able-to-move thing.

Once the program got started, we enjoyed watching people dance, juggle, blow fire (no, seriously. It was using magic, but still, really cool), and play the piano they'd wheeled out to the field. Jade performed a song she'd written on her guitar. It brought tears to my eyes as it told of a boy and a girl who were never meant to be together.

Katy's dance class filled the stage as they danced to anything from hip hop to ballet. She came out after and did a solo. I was in awe as she did splits and leaps through the air. Her dance brought a standing ovation, and she bowed with a huge grin on her face.

Heidi and Ashley performed a ballad that earned them several whistles from the boys in the crowd. Their voices harmonized perfectly as they sang a cappella.

The night was chilly, and Luke draped his coat over my shoulders. He left his arm around me, pulling me toward him. I laid my head on his shoulder, enjoying the closeness. I didn't know why I was so lucky to find this boy who cared so much for me.

Near the end, I was surprised to see Liz stand and move to the front to talk to Sheri. She went up on the makeshift stage and nodded at Max, who was sitting at the piano. He started a classical piece, and Liz began what she did best—she painted. Only this time, it wasn't on canvas. She combined her art with fire and painted in the sky. No fireworks display could compare to the magic she performed that night. She added ice or wind where it was needed. Flowers burst into life, and cities grew in the night sky.

The song ended, along with the magic, and the crowd sat in stunned silence. Tears ran down my cheeks at the beauty, and I jumped up to clap for her.

Luke joined me, and the rest of the campers cheered wildly. Liz sobbed on stage, frozen, as she got calls begging for her to do more. I hurried forward and helped her back down to sit by Luke and me.

Everyone stood and went to grab sticks for S'mores while Liz sobbed into my arms. When she finally composed herself, she sat up.

"I'm sorry. I don't know what got into me."

"Liz, that was the most beautiful—" My throat caught and I had to clear it. "Where did you learn to do that?"

She looked at her hands. "I live out on a farm, and there are fields all around me. When I can't take being cooped up in my house, I go out and paint the sky. My dad told me to stop doing it, but tonight, I just wanted to share *something*. That was the only way I knew how to do it." She buried her face in her hands. "I'm so embarrassed."

Luke pulled her into his arms. "Liz, you have a talent no one else has. Don't be embarrassed by it." He nodded at Max, and gently moved her into his arms. Max led her away from the campfire, talking softly to her.

Luke turned to me and shook his head. "That was . . . phenomenal. I hope she keeps it up." He picked up a stick and a marshmallow and handed them to me.

"Thanks." I put the marshmallow on the stick and followed him to a fire pit. "And here I thought it was cool to open locks or change the appearance of a dress." I laughed.

"Hey, those are impressive. Most people can't do that. Although, I think you can do a lot more than that now."

"Yeah, thanks to this camp. And to you." I blushed, but I meant it. He'd helped me learn more in just a few lessons than I could have ever learned on my own.

"I didn't do much. I just taught you to channel it. You did the rest on your own." He popped his toasted marshmallow in his mouth and licked his fingers.

I yelped when my marshmallow started on fire. I blew it out, admiring the burnt, crispy covering. "Ah, just the way I like it." I waited for him to finish with his and then we went to get chocolate and a cracker. The flavors burst in my mouth when I bit into the gooey treat.

"Now, watch this." He took another marshmallow and put it on a toothpick. He flicked his hand to start a tiny fire on his fingertip. He roasted the marshmallow and let the flame go out.

"Whoa, that's cool." I tried the same thing, making sure to let only a little magic through. I roasted mine and let go of the flow. "I think I'm in trouble now that I know how to do this. My hips will never be the same." I popped it in my mouth.

He chuckled. "Yeah, although you probably don't want to be doing it in your house. And your neighbors might look at you strangely if you did it in your backyard."

"Good point." We each had one more and then wandered off toward my cabin. We sat on the step and watched everyone walk by. The night sky was filled with millions of stars. A cool breeze started up, making me shiver. "Be right back." I ran into the cabin and grabbed a blanket to wrap around us.

Luke was on the phone, pacing back and forth when I came back out. I waited for him to finish, trying not to pay attention to what was going on, but his raised voice kept pulling me in. He finally hung up and came to sit by me, his shoulders stiff.

"Everything okay?" I pulled the blanket around us.

He shook his head. "No. They want you to leave camp, saying it's too dangerous for you to be here. I told them you have nowhere to go and camp was safe as long as they could bring in a couple more people, but they didn't want to listen."

"They want me to leave?" I felt like I'd been slapped. He was right—I had nowhere to go. At least, nowhere I wanted to be. I had two more days before I was supposed to go home, and I really didn't want to face Julie or the girls sooner than necessary.

"They finally gave in. If this woman sticks by what she said, you should be fine until the end of camp. I'm not sure if I trust her, though."

"I know I don't." I shivered, and Luke pulled me closer.

"You'll be fine. We'll just keep you away from Nick again tomorrow. I'd better get going, though. Lights out and all that." Luke stood and pulled me up, then leaned down and kissed me softly. But I put my arms around his neck and kissed him harder.

Luke looked dazed when he finally pulled away, and I could hardly breathe. Wow. That was … wow.

He brushed his hand against my cheek. "You have a good night and sleep well. Please make sure you walk with Jade or someone to breakfast, and I'll see you there. I'll stay here until I know Jade and everyone else are back." He kissed me one more time and opened the door for me.

"Okay. Night, Luke." I floated into the cabin and went straight to my room to drop off my blanket. The other girls were still gone, so I was left alone to daydream. After brushing my teeth, I dragged myself to bed and drifted to sleep. My dreams that night were of me and Luke riding off on large white horses toward our new castle.

Chapter Fourteen

The day before the competition dragged on slowly. I wanted to be out playing sports, but it seemed like every time I turned around, Nick was there, glaring. He never said anything. I stayed right next to my roommates doing arts and crafts or attempting musical instruments. Katy invited me to her dance class, but I just laughed and told her she didn't want me near the building.

The mermaids were busy swimming back and forth and flipping up in the air. Apparently they would be competing as well. I caught a few nasty looks from them as I passed by, and I decided to walk a little faster. Wow, they could hold a grudge.

By that afternoon, I'd made enough crafts to last a lifetime, and my heart ached to be outside playing baseball.

Luke showed up at the arts building. "Hey, you want to practice some archery?"

I jumped out of the chair. "Yes! I mean, let me clean this up and I'll be right out." I quickly washed the brushes and turned to Liz. "Thanks for hanging out. See you at dinner?"

She looked up from her painting of a barn with an old tractor next to it. "See you there."

I skipped toward the archery fields, making Luke laugh.

"You were that bored?" he asked.

"You have no idea. I'm usually fine doing stuff like this, but knowing they're playing baseball without me was killing me."

"I'm sorry. I'm just trying to keep you safe." He handed me a bow and took one for himself.

"Where have you been all day?" I asked, finding a spot in front of a fifty-yard target. If I was going to do this, I needed to practice.

"Around. Mostly keeping an eye on Nick from a distance. He seems like a normal guy. He jokes with the few friends he has and he was here shooting a while ago, which is how I knew it was safe now."

"I'm sure he's fine with everyone else. He just doesn't like me."

"That's what I don't get. He has to be working for the woman, but how? And why? It just doesn't make sense." He took the first shot this time, hitting right in the center.

I took my turn, making sure to pull back farther on the string so I could hit the target. My arrow landed just below Luke's.

"Great job!" He took his turn, and we continued that way until we were both out of arrows. My arms felt like jelly and were screaming at me to stop.

A few of mine had hit the ground in front of the straw bales, but most had hit the target. I was thrilled. We decided to try the hundred-yard target, but I wasn't too hopeful that I would come anywhere close to it.

I let Luke go first because I knew we'd have to go searching for my arrows. Once he was done—hitting the target every time and getting a few in the bull's-eye—I stepped up and lifted my bow higher than normal, like I'd watched Luke do. The first three weren't even close. The next couple hit the bottom of the hay bale, and then I finally managed to get the rest in the circle.

"See, you can totally do the competition tomorrow." Luke started toward the target, and I ran to catch up.

"I guess so. What's the worst that could happen?" I picked up my arrows and put them in the quiver on my shoulder.

"They could laugh you out of the camp? You could be so embarrassed, your face would stay red forever?" He ducked away from my fist and ran.

I chased after him, laughing. I conjured up a ball of snow and chucked it at him, hitting him in the back of his head. He fell to the ground and acted like he couldn't get up.

He rolled over, groaning. "Where did you learn to do that?"

"I don't know. I just needed something to throw, and that's what came to mind." I held my hand out and he took it, pulling himself up.

He rubbed the back of his head and pulled ice away from his hair. "That was awesome. But seriously, a snowball?"

"Hey, it could have been mud." I took my arrows from him. Forming that ball had been totally spur of the moment—I would have to figure out how I did it so I could do it again. I barely felt the familiar ache of using the magic. Strange—maybe I would feel it later.

We left the archery area and headed in for dinner. It was being held earlier that night so we could get rest for the next day. The lodge was louder than usual, with everyone excited about the competition. I was quiet, content to listen to everyone else. But then I looked up to see Nick staring at me again, and the peace I'd felt was gone.

I stood up, surprising my friends. "Um, I want to go read a book before bedtime. See you guys at the cabin."

"I'll go with you. Liz, will you grab my plate?" When Liz nodded, Jade followed me to the door.

"You didn't have to leave. Peter looked like he was coming over to talk to you." I nodded my head toward him.

She hesitated. "No, I need to go with you. There's no way I'm letting someone get you again."

"Look, Nick's right there. I'm fine." I didn't feel fine, though. I was edgy. Something wasn't right, and it really bothered me.

"You don't know for sure it's him, though. It's not safe."

Luke came up behind Jade. "I'll go with her—it's all good. But we need to go soon. You're starting to attract attention, just standing here in front of the garbage can."

Jade bit her lip. "Are you sure? You can't go in the cabin."

"Then I'll keep watch outside like I've done the last couple of nights." He took my hand. "Come on, Syd."

I waved at Jade and left the lodge, feeling embarrassed. I didn't like having to be guarded everywhere I went.

"Thanks for saving Jade. She wants as much time with Peter as she can get." And of course, we'd be leaving Saturday morning, but I could see Luke after this. Or at least, I hoped so.

"Hey, it's my pleasure. Sorry I didn't sit with you— I was on the phone. It seems your dad is showing signs of waking up."

I grinned, a weight suddenly lifted off my shoulders. "Seriously? How do they know? Do you know where he is?" I didn't want the surge of happiness that flowed through my body. It was too good to be true.

"He's at a hospital that's hidden away. The doctors say he's been mumbling something over and over."

"Do you know what it is?" I asked, hoping for a clue to help him. It was good to know that Dad was in a place where Julie couldn't get to him.

"Arabelle? Something like that."

I gasped. "Arabella?" Tears welled up in my eyes. He hadn't talked about her by name in years.

"You know her?" He turned to me and wiped away a tear that had fallen.

"That's my mom. She died when I was little. He was heartbroken—I think he still is."

"I'm so sorry." He pulled me into a hug. "How did she die?" he asked quietly.

I shook my head. "I'm not sure. It was sudden. There wasn't even a body at the funeral. Daddy doesn't know, but I checked. I was only four, and I wanted to see her again."

"He never told you what happened?"

"No. I never asked. I was too scared to know the answer." I wiped my eyes and walked toward my cabin. "I want to see my dad."

"I know you do—I don't blame you. He was on a

trip at the time, so you'll have to take a plane to get there. Don't worry—he's fine."

"I hope so. I don't want to be around my stepmom without him." I shuddered.

Luke was silent for a moment. "Why did he remarry if he was so heartbroken about your mom?"

I shrugged. "I don't know—I never understood. A few years back, he came home with a new wife and daughters, and announced that he was married. It was strange. Like some sort of weird curse was put on him or something. He was in a daze for a while, but the more time he spent away from the house, the more aware he became."

"Are you sure he isn't under a curse?"

I laughed. "I pray every day that it will be broken, even though there isn't one. I think he's realizing just how rotten she is, but now he's kind of stuck with her."

"That doesn't sound like a fun life." He walked up the steps to the cabin. "Now, you go in and get some sleep, and I'll be right out here if you need anything."

"Thank you." I kissed him on the cheek before opening my door. "I think sleep is exactly what I need right now."

"Sweet dreams." He sat down on the step and gazed out over the lake. I smiled to myself, confident that Luke would help if he saw anything.

The trumpet sounded before the sun was fully up the next morning. I stumbled out of bed and quickly showered and dressed to go grab some breakfast. The other girls were yawning and grumpy, which made me realize just how wide awake I felt. What had I even dreamed about the night before?

After breakfast, everyone piled onto the buses. It was loud inside, with everyone so excited for the day, but I just watched out the window, nervous. I hadn't seen Luke that morning, so I wondered if he'd noticed anything last night.

Just before we were ready to leave, Luke ran up, looking through the windows before finally getting in to the last bus. I sat up straighter and searched for anyone that could be a threat to me, but everyone was busy talking and I didn't see anything unusual.

We headed toward the other camp, and my stomach tied into even more knots. I closed my eyes, envisioning everything I had to do to hit the target in archery. That was the event I was most worried about.

The bus slowed and turned onto a different road. I opened my eyes to see a camp similar to ours. The flag above the lodge was red, with a knight in armor riding a horse. We stopped near the lodge, and I waited for my turn to get out. I was ready to compete, even if it was just to get it over with.

We formed lines and headed toward the field located behind the lodge. Everyone "ooh"ed and "ahh"ed at the setup of the camp as we went around the corner, but I stopped, my heart pounding wildly. I knew this place. The area was decorated like a Renaissance fair—the same fair from my dreams. The only difference was the people. I'd been alone before.

Campers jostled me as they hurried toward the different booths. We were supposed to sign up for the events, so everyone headed for the desk where several counselors sat.

Jade ran up to me. "Isn't this amazing? They even have costumes if you want to dress up. Come on!" She pulled on my arm, not waiting for me to answer.

"Jade, wait. I can't play baseball in a dress!" I laughed at her excitement, letting go of my fear just a little.

"Oh, right. But as soon as you're done, you'll have to come back and change."

I waved and ran to find the rest of my team. We met at the field, and I watched for Nick as we started our warmups. I wanted to get the game over with so I could practice my archery.

Luke jogged up. "There you are. I've been looking everywhere for you."

"Sorry. I saw you get on a different bus. I didn't have any way of letting you know where I was."

"That's what our phones are for." He looked more serious than I'd seen him since we got to camp. "Look, you need to stick with me or one of your friends as much as possible. You were right—I caught Nick near your cabin a few times. I would chase him off only to find him near it again. I had to go check in, and by the time I got back, you were gone."

"Well, I'm here now. Thanks for keeping watch. I was finally able to have normal dreams."

"I'm glad you slept. That makes one of us." Luke yawned. I could see faint rings under his eyes.

"Why didn't you sleep?" I hadn't meant for him to stay up all night.

"Too much going on." He looked toward the baseball diamond. "They need a team captain. That's you."

"Me? When did I become captain?" I was sure Nick would have insisted on taking that role, and I was perfectly okay with that.

"Before we left. No one told you?" He nudged me toward the field, and since no one argued, I ran out to meet the other team.

The ump gave us a rundown of the basic rules and then had me call heads or tails. I called heads and got it, so we would be going out to field first.

Luke helped me tell everyone their positions, and then leaned over to me. "Nick didn't show. I don't like this."

"I don't either. And that's not all, but I'll tell you later." I jogged to first base, and the game started. I wasn't going to think about anything else. Right now, I was here to play ball.

The sun was hot, but the slight cool breeze kept us from burning up. Luke struck out the first batter. Then the second batter hit the ball out to center field, getting him to first base. The third batter hit a foul ball that I was able to get under and catch.

As the game continued, my focus shifted between the plays and glancing around to see if I could find Nick. I hadn't seen him on the bus, but there were three others he could have taken. How his absence wasn't discovered during roll call, I didn't know, but it wasn't like him to miss a game.

We won by three runs. We cheered for the other team and then headed off to our next events. For Luke and me, it was the archery tournament.

My hands were shaking and my stomach so tied in knots, I thought I was going to lose my breakfast. Luke was quiet and distant, which didn't help much.

I somehow made it through the first round of the tournament and started getting my mind ready for the next round when I heard my name being called and found my roommates in the crowd, cheering. It helped me feel better, and I was able to pass through that round as well.

"You're doing a fantastic job. Just remember what we went over." Luke stood next to me, watching the others take their turn.

"Got it." I paused. "Is everything okay?"

"I'm fine. I'm just letting nerves get to me." He stepped up to the line and sent the arrow flying. It hit in the center of the bull's-eye.

"Nice one!" I called. I stepped forward, pulled back on my string, and took a deep breath. I knew what I had to do. I aimed carefully and let go. The arrow hit the target, but not inside the circle. It was disappointing, but I knew I was lucky to get as far as I had.

I joined my roommates to watch Luke finish up the competition.

"I didn't know you could do that, Syd," Ashley said.

"I couldn't until this week. I have a good teacher." My face burned when the girls burst into giggles.

"I'd learn too if I had a teacher like that." Heidi giggled again. "Oh! I need to head off to the hundred-meter relay." She took off, followed by Ashley, who would be running a couple of other races.

"I'll be back too. I promised I'd help my friend with a few dance moves. See you in a while." Katy ran off in the other direction leaving me alone to watch Luke. Once he was done, other campers surrounded him to congratulate him on his win, so I decided to go find Jade. She wasn't competing, so she must be over among the booths somewhere.

I wandered around, looking at the different shops the campers had set up. It was pretty amazing. Some of them had made jewelry to sell, while others were selling clothes. I couldn't find Jade, but what I did find chilled me to my core.

The fortune-teller's tent was exactly where I'd found it in my dream. Goose bumps ran down my arms as I recognized the runes on the tent and the tattered appearance of the sign above the door. Desperate to get away, I turned and ran, keeping an eye out for Jade and making sure I didn't run into Nick.

At the end of the row of tents, I took a right and stopped, my stomach clenching in fear. The tent stood there, beckoning me to come in. No. This couldn't be happening. I'd just left it behind, so why was it here? I pushed past the crowd of campers waiting in line for food and took another right. There was it was again. My palms were sweaty and my heart pounded. I ran my hand through my hair and gripped it, trying to gain some sense of control.

After trying to get away from the tent only to have it appear another time, I took a moment and let anger replace the fear. I cursed under my breath and went straight for the tent. If it wasn't going to leave me alone, I would just take it head-on. It had to be part of the camp ambiance, right? What else could it be? I was just scaring myself for no reason.

But when I entered the tent, I knew I'd been here before. The same smells of incense burned my nose, and the décor was exactly the same.

"Ah, there you are," a voice said in the dimly lit room. It was the old woman I'd seen in my dream of the fair. This was too creepy.

"What are you doing here?" I demanded. I had to hold tightly to that anger or I would lose to the fear that threatened to overwhelm me.

"I have come to tell your fortune, of course." She gestured to the crystal ball in front of her. A deck of cards and a cup of bones sat to the side.

"You already did, and it came true. I lost my dad in that stupid dream. I don't want to hear any more—I can't lose anything else. I only came in here because I had no choice."

"You always have a choice." Her smile showed several missing teeth. She picked up the cards sitting next to the ball.

"Not when I see the tent every time I go around the corner." I clenched my fists at my sides, determined not to let my emotions get the best of me.

"Sit, sit. Let's find out why it's so important for you to come see me." She shuffled the cards and set four in front of her. She turned over each one, nodding and mumbling to herself. "Ah, you seek for a way to save your father, but there is much more to the prison where you find yourself. There is a way to break free, but you must use the power you have to do it. The time is coming."

I sat down in front of her and leaned forward, hope fluttering nervously in my chest. "What do you mean?"

"I only know what the cards tell me, but I warn you that things must happen soon. Time is running out."

I glanced between her and the cards. "You know all that from those cards? How in the world does that work?" I'd seen tarot readers on TV and never believed they could predict anything. But she'd been dead on before. Why not now?

"They only tell me what I need to see." She shuffled them again and waved me away. "Your fortune is done. Now go."

"But that wasn't a fortune. At least, not one that makes any sense." I stood, frustrated. That was more of a tease than anything.

She shrugged. "I have nothing else."

I left the tent more confused than I was before, but when I turned the corner, I was thankful *not* to see the fortune tent in front of me yet again. What I did find was a stage, where Jade was performing one of her songs. I followed the gathering crowd and cheered when she was done.

Jade performed a few more songs before she bowed and headed toward me. "Hey, how did everything go?"

"I got to the last target, and we won our baseball

game. So I guess we did pretty well." I smiled, glad to have something else to think about. "I enjoyed your songs. Did you write them, too?"

"Yep. I don't do sports, but I can come up with lyrics pretty quickly. I noticed that a few of the other campers were singing, so I decided to join in."

"It was awesome." My stomach rumbled. "Think we can find some food here?" I looked around for the fortune-teller's tent to make sure it hadn't snuck up on me again.

"I think I saw noodles one aisle over. Come on." We wandered through the crowd and found a few places to buy our food for lunch. Jade bought herself some barbecued chicken, and I grabbed a taco and some soda. We went over and sat by the stage to watch Katy's group perform while we ate. Once we were done eating, we threw away our wrappers and wandered through the booths.

"Hey, did you get your fortune told?" I asked. The lady was kinda creepy, but I wondered if it was just because I'd dreamed about her.

Jade perked up. "There's a fortune-teller? That's awesome. I've been dying to know if Peter's going to call when we get home, or if this is just a camp fling. I found out he lives pretty close to me."

"I'm sure he will at some point." I wandered through the area where I'd thought the fortune-teller's tent was, but it was nowhere to be seen. "That's weird. I'm not finding it anywhere."

"Oh, well. I guess things are better left up to fate, right?" She stopped to look at some beads and picked out a long strand of light blue pearls, then pulled out her money and paid for the necklace.

I picked out a strand that had alternating dark purple and white stones on it and handed over the cash Dad had given me to find something nice. This would work with a few of the shirts he bought me before I left.

I bought a tie tack and a pen for Dad just as the whistle blew for us to go to the campfire. I realized I hadn't seen Luke since I'd left him at the archery competition, so I looked around for him. He sat with his friends, laughing when they made a joke, but otherwise staying quiet. What had happened last night?

The awards for the day were handed out, and I got a medal for winning the baseball game. Heidi came in third in her race, and Ashley had won one of her events. The overall winner trophy went to our camp, meaning that we would be hosting the competition the next year.

It was late when we were told to head back to the buses. I stayed with Jade and the other girls so I wouldn't have to ride with people I didn't know on the way back to camp.

I really didn't want to go home the next day—I actually had friends who liked me for who I was instead of hating me for who my stepsisters made me into.

We were able to sleep in our decorated rooms one last time and would be switching them back the next morning. I sprawled out under the covers of my huge bed and stared up at the canopy. It felt so much like home, even if I'd only created it in my head.

I wasn't supposed to be back here. I was supposed to have another day. I growled in anger, just wanting one more night's sleep. I spun at the movement behind me and saw the woman standing there, watching me.

"What do you want?" I clenched my hands into fists.

"You brought yourself here this time. I would have thought you'd stay away while you still could," she said. "But while you're here, do you have something for me?"

I stomped my foot, frustrated. "You want something to make you happy? Fine." I pulled on the stone below me and began making small stairs that curled around a box. On top of those stairs, I made another set, and then another. "You seem to like stairs so much—here. Take these and leave me alone."

The woman stared at me for a second before clicking her tongue. "It's a shame you lost your temper. I may have to double your price. You bore me today. Come back when you have something worth my time."

Chapter Fifteen

It was much easier to shift the room back to the simple place it had been than to make it my own. I finished packing and waited for everyone else to finish theirs.

Now that it was time to leave, I was anxious to go home. I wanted to figure out where my dad was, which meant I'd have to sneak out of the house.

I hugged Katy, Liz, Heidi, and Ashley goodbye with promises to write and meet up again the next year. Jade and I went to find our bus, and I helped her put her luggage in the baggage compartment. Jade didn't live too far away, so she made me promise we would do something together. I hoped it would happen, but I didn't think it was something Julie and the girls would let me do. Luke nodded at me as he passed by my seat. He was chatting quietly on the phone and found a seat by himself in the back.

"Is everything okay with you two?" Jade asked, nudging me.

I shrugged. "I don't know. He was really quiet at the competition, and I haven't seen him since. I don't know what's going on with him."

"Weird." Jade pulled a magazine out of her bag, and we spent the ride home taking quizzes and commenting on the outfits they were advertising.

No one was there to meet me when we got to the parking lot, which didn't surprise me. I waved at Jade as she left and took out my phone to call a cab.

Luke pulled his Honda Pilot up next to where I stood and climbed out. "Do you have a ride?"

I shook my head, feeling my face burn. "No, Julie either forgot or doesn't care. I was just finding a number for a taxi."

"Don't worry about it—I can give you a ride. I don't live too far from you." He smiled and gestured toward his car.

I looked up at him, surprised. "You know where I live?"

"Our dads work together, remember?" He picked up my luggage and put it in the trunk of his car. I shrugged and climbed in front.

"So now that camp is over, do you have anything exciting to look forward to?" Luke asked, turning onto the highway.

"Not really. I'll be cooking, cleaning, mowing the lawn, more cooking, and then whatever else Julie comes up with." I stared out the window, watching as we left the trees and drove down into the valley.

"That sounds … exciting." He laughed. "Surely you can do something fun in between all that work."

I shrugged. "That depends on when Dad wakes up. If it was up to Julie or my stepsisters, I'd never leave the house except to do yard work." I would have mentioned my party, but I was pretty sure Julie would find a way to have it canceled.

"Maybe I can help you escape and go to a movie." He turned right and continued into town.

I stared at him. Was he asking me on a date? "That would be great." Not that Kaylee or Sarah would let that happen. Not with how much Sarah had been dying over Luke at the restaurant.

"Great—I'll give you a call. I'll be pretty busy this summer, too. Dad has me in charge of his car dealership here while he's off taking over for your dad." He turned onto my road. "I don't mind, though. I get to test drive all kinds of fun cars."

"That sounds good to me. If I do get out, I'll get to ride my ancient bike."

Julie's car was gone when we pulled up to the house, and I sighed in relief. I wouldn't have to put up with her for a bit.

"Thanks for the ride." I moved to pull my bag out of the trunk, but Luke grabbed it first.

"Hey, no problem. I'll call you when I hear anything about your dad. And of course, to set up a time to go see the movie I promised you." He leaned down and kissed me goodbye.

"That would be great." I couldn't help grinning as I waved and hurried into the house, excited for a little quiet time until Julie got back.

That was, until I got inside. I was pretty sure they hadn't done a single thing for themselves while I was gone. Dishes were piled high, and leftover takeout food sat all over the table. For people who loved to shop, I was surprised at how little they knew about caring for their stuff.

I went to the laundry room and started a batch of my clothes before going back to my bedroom to finish unpacking. I flopped on the bed, deciding to rest until they got home. It had been a long week, and I didn't feel like waiting on them hand and foot. I was totally absorbed in my book when I heard the door slam open.

"Sydney, get in here now! I know you're home." Julie's shrill voice rang throughout the house.

Yeah, it was home sweet home all right. I put my book away and slowly walked into the kitchen where Julie stood, fuming.

"We're hungry, and this kitchen is a mess. Get it

cleaned up and make some spaghetti. Oh, and we have laundry that needs to be done. Get moving."

"Yes, ma'am," I muttered under my breath.

"What did you just say?" She narrowed her eyes.

"I said, 'Yes, ma'am.' Isn't that what I'm supposed to say to the person bossing me around?" I grabbed the pots from the sink and moved them over so I could get to the cups.

Julie came close and yanked me around, forcing me to look at her. "Don't you give me that lip. I don't know what you were taught at camp, but here, you respect your parents. Now get to work." She let go and stormed toward her room.

I filled the dishwasher, not caring to keep the noise down when I set the dishes in the racks. Once it was started, I got to work on the spaghetti. In the time it took for me to get that ready, Kaylee and Sarah had made another list of things for me to do. I was tempted to use my newly tamed magic on one or both of them, but refrained. This was my dad's house, and I didn't want it destroyed by a rogue fireball.

I set the spaghetti on the table and gathered up the laundry, giving the girls and Julie enough time to figure out that dinner was ready. When they didn't come, I grabbed a plate from the cupboard and served myself. I wanted to get out of there before I was told to do more chores.

Kaylee came out of her room, holding a pink top. "Syd—what do you think you're doing? You can't eat without us." Her whining caused the other two to come running.

"I was just eating quickly so I could get out of your way. I have lots of other stuff I have to do, remember?" I took my last bite and stood to put my plate in the sink. The girls tortured me with more chores while I scrubbed the floors and watered the plants that were nearly dead. I wanted to make sure the house was perfect for whenever Dad woke up. I wondered if Julie even knew Dad was missing.

It was past midnight by the time I felt like the house was in good shape, and I dropped into bed, exhausted.

I groaned when I realized where I was. She hadn't been joking when she told me I had two nights off. Well, I wasn't going to play the game. I was tired, and I just wanted to sleep. I pulled the cloak from around my neck and made a bed on the landing. I wished there was a blanket cupboard somewhere.

Suddenly, I heard a pop, and in front of me, there was a table holding a thick, soft blanket. What the . . .? I picked it up and looked around, searching for an explanation. This had never happened before. The blanket was just exactly what I'd asked for. Was this just like changing my room at camp? Hesitantly, I asked for a pillow, and one appeared right where the blanket had been. I'd never been able to do this before. I asked for random items, and they appeared on different parts of the landing. I could get used to this.

I decided it was time to change the décor of this ugly, creepy staircase, so I pushed out, picturing a nice yellow paint with flowers along the walls. When I opened my eyes, the landing looked the same as it did in my mind. I picked a daisy out of a nearby vase and smelled it. The scent was strong, and much sweeter than the mustiness I was usually stuck with while here.

I wondered if I'd be able to find the doorway that led to my dad's chamber again and closed my eyes to concentrate on what it looked like—

I snapped awake to Julie shaking me. The dream had been awesome and I wanted to go back, but from the glare on Julie's face, it wasn't going to happen.

"Where's your dad?" she asked.

"What?" I glanced over to see that was eight thirty in the morning. I'd slept in? It felt like I'd only been asleep for a few minutes.

"Your dad. Where is he? He won't answer his phone or his emails. What's going on?"

"He's probably in meetings." I grabbed my pillow and put it over my head. "Would you please let me sleep?"

"Oh, no, you don't. Get out of bed and make us some breakfast. You already had your vacation at camp. Now that you're home, you have work to do. I want some breakfast, and I've been waiting for hours."

I lifted my pillow. "Hours? It's early. And besides, I cleaned the house last night. Make your own breakfast."

Julie reeled back as if I'd slapped her. "What did you just say to me?"

I sat up, fuming. "You heard me. Make your own breakfast. My word, what did you do while I was gone?"

"Enough. Get out there and make my breakfast, or you'll wish you'd never been born." Her voice dripped with venom.

"Oh, like you have that power," I snapped.

Julie got down into my face and stared into my eyes. "You *will* make me breakfast. Now."

Without thinking, I climbed out of bed and went in to the kitchen. I shook my head, wondering what had just happened. I pulled out the ingredients for smoothies and threw them into the blender. Once they were mixed, I poured the smoothies into cups and wandered back to my room. I wanted back in that dream. I had to find out if I could use my powers to find doors, or even to get out of there.

The pounding on my door knocked me out of my thoughts. "Sydney, get back out here this instant. You have cleaning to do for the ball."

Right. The ball. I opened the door to find Julie standing there, arms folded. "The ball isn't for a week. And besides, I cleaned everything last night. How you three messed it up so badly is beyond me."

She glared. "That's no way to speak to your . . . mother. The backyard needs to be mowed, and the shrubs need to be pruned. It's a mess, and our lawn boy quit."

"You will never be my mother, so don't even try. And what happened to Andy? Did Kaylee and Sarah drive another one off with their never-ending flirting?" This happened at least once a month during the summer. They would sit outside and flirt with the lawn boys enough that the guys would get annoyed and quit. I grabbed some socks and my sneakers, thankful to have a reason to get out of the house—even if it was to do yard work.

Julie stiffened. "He said he wasn't being paid what it was worth. Fifteen dollars a week is plenty. I'll be calling his mother to complain today."

"Oh, brother. Like that's going to do anything." I brushed past her and went outside to find the mower. The lawn was already short, but Julie had an obsession with making sure every blade was exactly the same height. Too bad she wouldn't do the work herself.

Our lawn was massive, so it would take a couple of hours to finish the mowing. I was about halfway done when I felt buzzing in my pocket. I turned off the mower and grabbed my phone.

"Dad?" I asked.

"No, this is Phil, your father's friend. He's waking up, and he's asking for you. We need you to come to the hospital as soon as possible."

I looked at the house to see Julie glaring at me from the large windows in our living room. "I can't leave yet. Not with Julie watching over my shoulder."

"We have someone coming to get you. Be ready." The phone went dead.

I started the mower again, feeling Julie's eyes on me. Phil had told me to be ready, but I knew what would be waiting for me when I got home if this didn't get done.

I pulled the mower into the garage and began pruning a shrub. My phone buzzed again.

"Hello?"

"Your stepmother is a charming woman, isn't she?" Phil sounded amused.

"You have no idea."

"Your ride is there, but you're going to have to sneak around the house and climb in. That is, unless you really did fall and break your arm and leg and are stuck in bed for the rest of the summer."

"*What?*" Instead of going up to the house, I rounded the side and peeked to find a sleek, cherry-red BMW in the driveway.

"That's what she told our driver. Are you almost there?"

"Yes, but Julie is out here, screaming at your guy."

Phil cursed softly. "Okay. Hang up—I'll find some backup."

I crouched down and listened to Julie screaming and raving about how horrible it was that they would try to torture her poor injured stepdaughter by asking her to come to the door. I rolled my eyes. Her fake sympathy for me was worse than when she treated me horribly. At least I knew that was sincere.

A car door slammed, and footsteps went up the walk. "Hello. Is Sarah home?"

My heart pounded in my chest. Luke? What was he doing here?

Julie's voice instantly changed. "Oh, goodness. Luke, right? I'll go get her."

I jumped up and ran for the car as soon as Julie went in the house. I slipped inside and ducked down just as I heard Sarah's shriek of excitement. I peeked over the edge of the window, curious what was going on.

"Luke, how wonderful to see you." She moved in closely. I was pretty sure she had no sense of personal space.

"I was . . . wondering if you'd like to go get ice cream."

"Of course." She grabbed on to his arm and practically dragged him to his car. I knew it was part of the plan, but it still hurt to see Luke with Sarah, her arm wrapped through his as they walked.

The driver climbed in the car where I hid and drove away. He said nothing until we were away from the house.

"Your stepmother is . . . quite something," he said, smiling into the rearview mirror. He had a slight accent that I couldn't place.

"Yeah, she is. Sorry you had to deal with that." I watched the stores go by for a few minutes. "So, where are we going?"

"California."

"Wait—what? How?" I knew Dad traveled, so this shouldn't have surprised me, but when he'd gotten the message about my cure, I thought it was somewhere local.

"That's where your father is. You'll be flying."

"I've never been there. I know nothing about it." I panicked. I wanted to see my dad more than anything, but just to be dropped off in a whole different state?

"You'll have an escort. It will be fine. Oh, and there is a change of clothes in the bag next to you, along with some cash for anything you might need on the way."

I raised an eyebrow. "You just happened to have an outfit for me?"

"Your house is watched at all times." He caught the look on my face and laughed. "Don't worry—it's only from the outside. Anyway, we saw you outside working and knew you'd need to change."

I looked down at the clothes I was wearing and

grimaced. Definitely *not* traveling clothes. And my hair was probably flying everywhere. "Um, thanks. I'll change at the airport."

"Very well." He pulled up to the sidewalk and hurried around to help me out. "Here is your ticket. Check in and go straight to the gate. Your escort will be there."

"How will—" I started.

"You'll know," he interrupted and tipped his hat. "Good luck. I hope your father wakes soon."

"Thanks." I ran in to the airport and stopped, trying to figure out where to go. I didn't need to check any luggage, so I went toward the security line. Thankfully, it wasn't long. Dad had complained about the wait several times.

I let the man go through my bag and stepped through the metal detector. It blared loudly, and I walked back through so they could scan me. The wand beeped at my pocket, and my face reddened as I pulled out a pair of small garden clippers I'd forgotten to take out before I left home. The security guard raised his eyebrows and pulled me aside.

"Would you care to tell me why you had these in your pocket?" He gestured to the clippers before throwing them in the bin.

"Garden work. I had to rush out of the house, and I didn't realize I still had them." I knew it sounded lame, but hey, it was the truth. I prayed he'd believe me.

Another guard hurried over and whispered in his ear, gesturing toward me. The first guard looked me up and down. "I'll let you through, but next time, leave the garden tools at home."

I sighed in relief. "Thank you. I will." I nodded at the second guard and rushed off to find a bathroom where I could change my clothes before catching my flight. I only had twenty minutes until I was supposed to board.

After finding an open bathroom stall, I went in and locked it. The clothes the guard had picked were surprisingly cute. There was a pink dress and purple leggings that fit perfectly. I shoved my dirty clothes in my bag and checked my appearance in the mirror before heading out.

I grabbed a book and some snacks from one of the stores, using the cash I was given, and then headed over to the gate. The driver had said I would recognize my escort, but no one was here. I was one of the first called to board, so I handed off my ticket and climbed on the small plane, glancing around one more time. I'd somehow scored a window seat near the front. The rows were crowded together, with only two seats on each side of the aisle.

Just as the doors were about to close, a woman stepped into the plane. It was Anne, the woman who'd helped me make the jewels in art class. She sat next to me, breathing heavily.

"Sorry about that. I couldn't get through security. The line was long—someone apparently brought in some clippers or something, and it made security pay more attention to everything."

"That was me. I'm sorry." Great. I would never live this down.

She laughed. "How did you do something like that? You'd think you'd remember you brought them with you."

"They were small, and I was too frazzled by everything that had just happened."

"It's okay. We got on the flight just fine. Now, I hope you don't mind, but I need to sleep. I get airsick if I don't."

"It's okay. I have a book I can read. And thank you for coming with me. I'm so embarrassed that I need someone to watch out for me everywhere I go."

"That's what we're here for." She leaned back and closed her eyes.

Still, it was strange to have people watching out for me. I had probably driven Luke crazy. He'd barely paid attention to me the last two days of camp, and I hadn't seen him since he'd given me a ride home. Well, until he came to take Sarah on a date.

I pulled out the book and tried to read, but my mind was too distracted by thoughts of seeing my dad. I wanted to go back into my dreams to find him, but I didn't know if I could sleep on the plane. Besides, I didn't know what happened to my body when I went into the dreams. I would hate to be running in place or something in public. I'd just have to wait and see him when we got there.

The flight was a short one, so we soon began our descent. My ears popped as I stood to stretch. I tapped Anne on the shoulder to wake her up, and she flinched and looked around.

"Okay, we should have a ride waiting for us." She yawned and led the way off the plane. We walked into the terminal, and Anne put her hand on my back and guided me forward.

"Are you Sydney?" the man asked. He was a handsome older man dressed sharply in a suit and tie.

"Yes. Who are you?" It came out sharper than I wanted it to, but I had been put in the hands of a lot of strangers lately.

"I'm Phil. We spoke on the phone." He reached out to greet me.

"Oh, hi. So, where is the hospital?" I shook his hand first, and then Anne did as well.

"We have an hour's drive. My car is parked just outside." He led the way and helped us into the backseat of a limo.

"Whoa." I stared at all the buttons and the leather seats. Dad had been in one a few times with business clients, but I hadn't had the chance.

"It was the only thing I could find on such short

notice that had dark windows and extra security features." He shut the door and climbed in front.

I turned to Anne. "Why do we need extra security?"

She looked uncomfortable, but shrugged. "Your dad is an important man, which means you are important as well. We're just taking precautions."

"Right." I watched as stores and homes passed by. I must have drifted off because when Anne nudged me, we were in a quiet neighborhood with a small hospital nestled among the trees. I climbed out, surprised at the salty scent in the air. I wondered how far we were from the ocean, but I didn't have a chance to ask before we were ushered into the building.

Phil walked past the front desk and down the hallway to a heavily guarded door.

A short, round nurse with graying hair hurried over. "The wires and monitors make it look worse than it is. Don't you worry—they're just there to make sure your dad is fine. He seems more awake than he has in several days. You can talk to him, but he probably won't answer."

I nodded. "Okay. Can I see him now?"

"Of course."

Phil showed a badge to the guards, and they let us pass through.

Dad lay in a bed in the center of the room. Even though I had been warned about the machines, it still made my stomach drop to see him there with wires all over him. I choked back a sob and ran to him. He looked a little pale, and he was sweating, but otherwise, he looked just like he was in a simple sleep. I took the hand that didn't have an IV in it and kissed it.

"Daddy?" I touched his face, surprised at how warm he was.

He jerked, but kept his eyes closed. "Syd . . . Arabella . . . trapped," he muttered.

My heart skipped a beat. "What, Daddy?" I leaned forward, hoping to get more out of him. When I didn't hear anything else, I turned to the nurses. "Has he said more than that?"

A nurse shook her head. "That's the most I've heard."

I stared at him, willing him to wake up. Wait—I had an idea. If I could change things around in my dreams, maybe *I* could wake him up.

"Can I have some time with him, please?"

"Of course. We'll give you a few minutes." The nurse ushered everyone out of the room, and I could hear her telling the guards not to let anyone in.

I waited until it was silent in the hall and then ran my hand along the edges of the door to freeze it shut with my magic. I needed more than just a few minutes. I stood next to my dad, but far enough away that I wasn't touching him. No need to take both parts of him with me into the dream, although I would do that next if this didn't work. I needed my dad back.

Chapter Sixteen

There was no chair to sleep in, so I had to roll up a blanket and make myself comfortable on the floor. I closed my eyes, willing myself back onto the stairs. There was a quick pull on my body, and then I stood on a landing. Perfect. Now which way was I supposed to go? Up was always good, so I climbed for several flights before stopping to catch my breath. I'd forgotten how quickly I tired when I was fully in the dream. When I had my energy back, I pictured the door I'd seen before and pushed on the memory, feeling the whoosh as the magic took effect. The door appeared in front of me and I cheered, then slowly opened it. No need to go barging in only to be eaten by a lion or something.

Dad was still lying on the table I'd seen him on

before. He seemed to be less solid, almost as if he were only partially in this world.

"Daddy?" I waited for a second. "Daddy? You need to go home. You need to wake up."

He stirred slightly, but continued to sleep. I growled in frustration and paced the floor. What was I supposed to do? But then memories of when I'd touched the cloth came back to me. It had taken a jolt to get me out of that dream. I bit my lip, wondering if it could work this time. Dad was big, so it would take a little bit more magic, but I was willing to try. I pulled the blanket off him and laid it on the floor.

I pushed and prodded him, but I couldn't get him to move. Something had to work—Dad needed to get out of here. Taking a step back, I conjured up as much wind as I could and shoved it at him, but it didn't do any good. It just ran over the top of him. Tears of anger ran down my face while I thought of something else to do.

There had to be a different way. Some kind of leverage. I took stock of the room and didn't find much to use except a tall candlestick that stood in the corner. The metal was pretty strong, so I got a good grip on it and shoved it underneath Dad. Taking a deep breath, I jumped and pushed down hard on the stick, making him roll onto his side and then off the table.

I fell with the momentum of the candlestick and landed with an *ooph*, and then blackness.

The beep of the heart monitor was the first thing I heard when I woke on the floor of the hospital room. The wind had been knocked out of me, so it took a second to pull myself up to standing. Someone pounded on the door. I quickly thawed the doorknob and opened it. Dad's nurse stood with her hand raised to knock again. Guards stood around her with their hands on their weapons.

"Hey, how's it going?" I gave the nurse what I hoped was an innocent smile while I was still trying to catch my breath.

The guards rushed in and searched the room while the nurse glared at me. "What happened to the door? We couldn't open it."

"Really? How odd." I turned at the sound of a groan coming from behind me. Dad was awake and looking around the room. Tears ran down my face as I hurried over. My plan had worked!

"Princess?" His voice was hoarse. I grabbed the water and helped him get a drink.

Nurses bustled around us, checking his blood pressure and all the other monitors. Dad lay back on his bed and closed his eyes. When things calmed down a little, he opened his eyes again and focused on me.

"You're really here?"

"Yes, I am." I took his hand and squeezed it.

"You should be at camp." He coughed and pointed toward the water by his bed.

I helped him take another drink. "Dad, you've been out for a week."

Dad's eyes widened and he coughed again. "How is that possible? I don't remember anything after meeting with Phil."

"It was the cloth you took from my room. Since you're not supposed to go into my dream, when you touched the cloth, you were stuck in limbo. No one could get you out."

He looked around the room at everyone standing there. "So how *did* I get out of it?"

"Um, you just woke up." My face burned, but I didn't want to admit that I'd pushed him off a table. Maybe I'd tell him when we were home. I turned to the nurse. "How long does he have to stay here?"

"We'll run a couple of tests to make sure there's no neurological damage from his coma, and then we can release him," a man said from the doorway. He walked over to the bed and held out his hand. "I'm Dr. Katz. I've been keeping an eye on your dad."

"Thanks for taking care of him." I watched Dad as he talked to the nurses. He seemed to be fine, by the way he joked with them.

The doctor leaned forward. "He mentioned Arabella several times. Did he happen to tell you why?" he whispered.

Dad looked over at us, eyes wide. "What did you say?"

The doctor cleared his throat. "You mentioned two names while you slept. Your daughter's, and an Arabella."

Dad rubbed his face, something he only did when he was agitated. "She was my late wife. But . . . I don't . . ." His confused looked changed to surprise. "I dreamed of her. It's been years since I've dreamed of her."

"We'll let you rest for a bit before we do any tests. Sydney, you're free to stay with your dad, but don't excite him."

"Thanks. I'll be careful." I waited for everyone to leave, then pulled up a chair and sat by the bed. "What did you see, Dad?"

He was quiet for a minute. "She was there. It was so real. She was calling to me, but I couldn't find her."

"She died, though. She couldn't have been there." Except that the stairs were a real place—the things that happened there were real, including the bruise I could feel forming on my rib from landing so hard.

Dad turned his face away. "I know. That's why I was so confused. I wanted it to be real."

"When you were asleep, you said 'trapped.' Is she trapped?"

He shook his head. "No. I remember getting word that she was gone."

"Dad, I learned more about the stairs while you were asleep. Did you know that Mom had made a deal with some lady so she could get pregnant with me?"

He looked at me in surprise. "Where did you hear that?"

"This old lady in the dream. She told me that's why I'm cursed. Mom had to run those stairs to pay off a debt, and when she died, I had to take over. For some reason, even though it was supposed to have been paid off, I'm still stuck there."

Dad muttered something under his breath. "That's why she was always so tired. I wish she'd told me. We could have taken care of this long ago."

"What do you mean?" Hope rose, and I tried to squish it down.

"Now we know what it is, so we can figure out a solution. Did the woman tell you what the payment was?"

I shook my head. "Only that it was paid off. But the lady is back, and she wants me to find something that will make her happy. She liked the jewels I made, but I'm still stuck."

Dad was silent for a moment. "That's strange." He found the remote for the bed and maneuvered it to a sitting position. "Can you help me? I've had enough sleep for a while."

I helped him stand and walk to the bathroom and then sat on the bed while I waited for him to come out.

My phone beeped, and I found a text message from Jade.

Hey, how's it going? Is everything okay?
Yeah. Dad's awake! Hopefully we'll be going home soon.
Oh, good. I was worried. Turn on the news.
I'm in California, though. What's going on?

Had something happened to my house while we were gone? I flipped through the channels, waiting for Jade to text back, and almost dropped my phone when I found a news channel. There was a missing person report—for me. I watched as Julie sobbed into the camera about how wonderful I was. She'd had her hair and nails done since I'd last seen her. I rolled my eyes. I'd only been gone since yesterday afternoon.

I changed the channel to watch cartoons and sat back in my chair. I felt more at peace than I had in days. I was back with my dad, right where I should be.

Chapter Seventeen

D r. Katz finally cleared Dad to go home after keeping an eye on him overnight. Anne had left not long after Dad woke up, figuring she wasn't needed anymore. The flight home was much more relaxing with Dad next to me.

We sat in the airport together, waiting for our ride. Dad noticed his car pulling up to the door and gestured for me to follow. One of his coworkers got out, waved, and left in another car.

"What do you think Julie's going to say when we show up at the house?" Dad asked.

"She'll flip out, fall all over you, and then decide to go shopping." I was just glad Dad was coming home with me. This way, Julie wouldn't freak out and make my life even more miserable.

As we drove, Dad talked to me about what had happened with the cloth, and I told him a little about camp. I mentioned being taken and how Nick was around the few times I'd felt like I was being watched.

"Are you sure he's the guy?" Dad's fists gripped tightly on the steering wheel.

"No. But the fact that he knew the woman was going to give me a couple of days off is too coincidental."

"I just wish I knew who she was and how she manages to live in that dream."

"What do you mean, she lives in it? I've only seen her a few times. It's Nick I see all the time. He's the one who grabbed me and pulled me in to talk to the woman. He's the one wearing the cloak I see on the stairs."

"If the woman you see in your dreams is the one who put the curse on you, she's most likely the one who's watching you, but from a distance. Nick may just be who she sends to take care of her dirty work."

"Maybe." Dad was probably right. She seemed to be the one in charge. If she *did* live in the stairs, there had to be other rooms, and I wondered if I'd be able to get into them.

Dad got a phone call, so I watched out the window as he talked about work stuff. I was relieved to be home—until we turned onto our street. There were news reporters outside my house. I groaned. This couldn't just end easily, could it? We pulled up, and Dad sat there for a moment with his mouth open.

"Uh, honey? Do you know what this is about?" Dad gestured toward the mass of cars.

"Me. Apparently Julie desperately misses me and wants the world to know. She was on the news last night."

He shook his head. "I don't know what I'm going to do with her."

"Kick her out? Make her do everything she's forced me to do?" I held up my hand when I saw that he was going to argue. "Dad, you should have seen what the house looked like when I got back from camp. I swear they're doing it to punish me."

"Maybe." He put his hand on the door handle. "Well, let's go face the media."

"Okay, fine." I could think of several other things I'd rather do than get out of the car. Like, getting a root canal, for instance. If Dad hadn't been there, I don't know what I would have done.

We counted to three, then opened the doors to the noise outside. The media swarmed us and began firing their questions. Dad stepped forward and cleared his throat.

"Sydney is fine. She joined me on vacation, and we just got back. Now, please leave our property so we can spend time together as a family."

He guided me into the house and we slammed the door, ignoring the reporters asking for more information.

"Well, that was exciting. I think I'll go nap now." I took a step toward my bedroom, wanting to avoid Julie.

"Nice try. Come on." He dragged me in to the living room, where Julie sat in a recliner, drinking tea and reading one of her fashion magazines. I could hear the music blasting from her headphones from where I stood. Yeah, she looked *really* concerned that we were gone.

"Honey? You're home! I was so worried about you." She set her drink down and scrambled out of her chair to throw her arms around my dad. "Where were you? I tried everything I could to get ahold of you."

"I was sick for several days and didn't have my phone by me." He pulled away from her. "Where are the girls?"

"They're out sho—looking for your daughter." She suddenly focused on me. "When did you get here?"

"I came in with Dad." I tried to act like it was no big deal, but inside, I was shaking. Her suspicious glare had made my mind totally freeze up.

She looked between the two of us. "What's going on? How did she know where you were when I didn't?"

"I'm sorry, but I was getting you something special when I fell ill and Sydney's number was at the top of my call list. I came home as soon as I was feeling better."

Her frown turned instantly into a wide smile. "You got me something? Where is it?"

Dad's eye twitched. "It's still being made. I'll be picking it up next week."

She sniffed, obviously disappointed that he didn't have the present with him. "I don't see why she even has a phone. We hadn't agreed on getting her one. And since she hasn't done her chores for today—"

"Stop. Now. She has done more than her fair share. She's my daughter, and I will allow her to have a phone if I see fit."

Julie jerked back. "*Your* daughter? I thought we worked together." She stormed away and slammed the door.

"I think you're going to pay for that one, Dad." I noticed the mess Julie had left around the chair she'd been sitting in and sighed. "Or I will." I picked up an envelope off the floor, but my dad stopped me.

"That's not your job. Could you please start some dinner? I'll go try to calm her down."

"Okay." I went in to the kitchen and pulled some chicken out of the fridge. I figured making Julie her favorite meal would help. Kaylee and Sarah walked in, carrying several bags.

"Wow, you two were looking really hard for me. Where did you go? The mall?" Not that I was surprised. They couldn't last a day without buying at least one thing. Kaylee scowled at me and continued to her room, but Sarah stayed behind.

"I see you're just fine. You caused a lot of trouble with your little runaway scheme." Sarah glared.

"Oh, brother. You got to be on TV. I would have thought you'd eat that right up." I pounded the chicken so I wouldn't reach over and strangle her.

"Yes, well, it messed up my date with Luke," she pouted. "He was just about to kiss me when Mom insisted that I had to get ready to be on the news."

I knew she was bragging about Luke on purpose, but I couldn't help pounding the chicken just a little harder than necessary. "Yeah? What makes you think that?"

"Oh, you could just tell by the way he looked at me. Besides, he's taking me out again tonight."

"What?" I wanted to scream, or cry, or something, but I wasn't going to let her get to me. I couldn't.

She leaned in. "He's taking me to dinner with Kaylee and Dillon. Oh, and Mom told me I could borrow your dress. You know, the dark blue one?"

I slammed down the tenderizer and glared at Sarah. "She can't let you wear that. It's mine." So much for not letting her bother me.

"Oh, but she can." Sarah smiled, knowing she'd had won because of the tear that escaped and ran down my cheek. Both girls knew that if they made me mad enough, I'd cry.

I seriously wanted to slap the smile off her face, but instead I turned and put the food in the oven, giving myself a chance to fight back the tears. When I turned, she was gone.

I chopped vegetables for the salad and waited for dinner to finish cooking while I set the table for Julie and Dad. There was no way I was going to eat with them while the girls were gone. I cleaned up behind myself and switched the laundry.

Once the chicken was out of the oven, I grabbed my

plate of food and knocked on Dad's door to tell him dinner was ready before hiding in my room. I nibbled at the chicken, not really in the mood to eat. I got up to turn on my stereo and stopped in my tracks. My closet was a mess. I rushed inside to find that the dress was gone. Sarah must have slipped in when I was cooking—I'd left the door unlocked.

I growled in frustration and stomped toward the kitchen. "Dad?"

Dad jumped up from the table. "What's wrong, honey?"

"Sarah has my dress. Again." I wanted to wipe the smug look off Julie's face. "You can't just let them borrow my clothes. They're mine."

Dad put his hands on my shoulders. "Honey, what are you talking about?"

I pointed at Julie, my hand shaking. "She told Sarah that she could use my dress. It's *my* dress. I . . . *made* that dress."

He looked down at Julie. "Did you really tell Sarah that?"

Her attempt at looking innocent was ruined by the sneer she directed at me. "Sarah was going somewhere nice tonight and needed something to wear. Sydney wasn't going, so I figured she wouldn't mind."

"Wait—where did they go?" Dad looked at her, confused.

Julie giggled. "You never notice anything, do you? Kaylee went out with Dillon tonight, and Luke took Sarah. She's been waiting to go out with him ever since you introduced them at the restaurant. Yesterday, he showed up on the doorstep and asked her out. He liked her so much, they're going out again."

I tried to swallow the lump in my throat. He was supposed to be *my* Luke. Was that why he was so distant those last two days? Was he done with me?

"That doesn't mean she can wear Sydney's dress. If she said no, that means no." Dad was trying to stay cool, but I could tell he was annoyed.

"It's a shame they've already left. Oh, well. No harm done."

Dad stared at her. "No harm done? You can't just let your girls run wild, doing what they want all the time. I saw how much they spent today. I'm going to have to cut off their credit cards if they don't stop wasting my money."

Julie slammed her hands on the table. "I will not have you speak to me like that. I have been worried sick about you since you left, and this is how you repay me?" She grabbed her purse and keys and left the house. The food I'd made lay forgotten on the table.

Dad rubbed his face with one hand and leaned back. "I wondered why she kept talking to me about random things. She was waiting for her daughters to make a clean getaway with your dress." He looked up at me. "I'm sorry, sweetie."

I dropped into the chair next to him. "It's not even the dress I'm upset about, though it nearly killed me trying to make it. It's the guy. Dad, I thought he liked me." I buried my face in my arms.

"I'm sure he does. Luke is just being nice as part of his cover. You'll see. Plus, you don't even know who asked who, right?"

I lifted my head. "I guess not. But still, thinking of them being together hurts." I stood and went to my room to get my food. Sitting with my dad at the table just felt right. I ignored the untouched plate of food sitting there where Julie had been.

"So, about that birthday." His eyes sparkled as he grinned at me. "Any ideas what you're going to wear?"

I picked at my food. "No, not since Sarah laid claim on my dress." I sighed. "Do I really need to have a party? No one's going to come."

"What about all the friends you met at camp? I thought you liked your roommates."

I perked up. "I can invite them?"

"Of course you can, princess. What's the point of having a party if you can't have your own friends come?"

"Sweet! I'm going to text them as soon as I get done eating." I stabbed my chicken with my fork and took a big bite.

Dad chuckled. "Slow down before you choke. While you're inviting your friends, I'm going to put in some calls and get things set up. I was thinking of holding the party at the country club. Will that work?"

"I thought Julie had it planned for here."

"She did? Well, where do you want it? It's your party." He pulled out his tablet.

I played with my fork, unsure what I wanted to do. Home would be easier and cheaper for my dad, but then I'd be the one doing all the work. "Let's do the country club, if that's okay."

"Anything for my girl. Okay, I'll send a message to schedule it for Saturday night and then start working on invitations. You write a list of who you want to invite. Texting to invite them is fine, but let's make this special for them too." He winked and stood.

"Thanks, Dad." I hopped up and threw my arms around him, and then ran to my room to start texting. Jade, Katy, and Heidi replied immediately. Ashley and Liz texted back a few minutes later, asking about bringing dates. I told them to invite whoever they wanted, but to make sure to let me know who was coming so I could tell my dad.

For the first time since my dad offered to throw me a ball, I was actually excited for it. This party really would be mine—and my dad would be there for it this year. I went online to go through a few dress ideas and heard a knock at the door.

"Come in," I called.

"Hey, sweetie. It's all set up. Did your friends reply yet?"

"Yes, they're all coming and bringing dates. Um, if that's okay." I ignored the fact that I didn't have a date yet.

"Of course. The more the merrier. And you need to figure out what you want to eat." He glanced at the computer screen. "That's a pretty dress. Is that the one you want?"

I shrugged. "I don't know. I haven't really thought about it until now." We went through the other pictures I'd saved and chose a couple to go look at later.

"All right, it's time for us to get to bed. Tomorrow is a busy day." Dad leaned down and kissed my cheek. "Careful on the stairs tonight."

"Thanks, Dad. I think I'll try to sleep again."

"Good luck." He left the room and shut the door behind him. I continued to look around online until I heard the girls come home from dinner. From the giggles, I assumed it went well. Time to pretend I was asleep so they wouldn't try to rub it in. I shut down the computer and tiptoed over to turn off the light.

"So, did he kiss you?" Kaylee asked outside my door.

"Yes," Sarah said, giggling. "It was amazing. And we're going out again this weekend."

I rolled my eyes. That wasn't obvious at all. I tried to keep out the noise with my pillow, but it was no use.

"What about Sydney's party, though? Don't you think he wants to go with her?"

Sarah's laugh grated on my nerves. "Of course not. Why go with her when he could have someone so much better? And did you see the way he kept looking at me? He obviously liked the dress better when I wore it."

Kaylee laughed. "Totally, but was there ever a question? Come on. I'm exhausted and need my beauty sleep. Dillon is taking me to the lake."

They wandered off, their voices muffled. Thankfully, it was ridiculous enough that their taunting rolled right off me. I knew they just did it to bother me, and I wouldn't give them that satisfaction.

The house was quiet an hour later, and I hurried out of my room to get ready for bed. Clothes and shoes were all over the floor of the bathroom, including my dress. I picked it up and opened the bathroom door to find Sarah standing outside, hand ready to knock.

"What are you doing with that?" she asked.

"Taking it back to my room. It's mine."

She sniffed. "Fine. Luke has seen me in it, anyway. I'll just have to find something else for this weekend." She pushed past me and slammed the door.

After the dress was hung up in my closet, I slipped into my bed and waited for sleep to come. Even the staircase was better than dealing with Kaylee and Sarah right now.

Chapter Eighteen

I wasn't alone. I hadn't felt this afraid here for a while, and I didn't know what was causing it. I ran, just wanting to get away from whoever was watching. When I couldn't go another step without fainting, I imagined a dresser and pushed it into a corner so I could hide. A closet would have been better, but I was too flustered.

Whoever it was came closer, stepping lightly. I curled up in a ball and hugged my knees, trying to get up the courage to peek out. I closed my eyes and breathed in slowly to calm myself down. I knew the person who'd trapped me here. I would use that knowledge to fight past the fear.

After counting to one hundred, I stood and faced the direction the person was coming from. I formed a fireball in my hand and waited. For extra effect, I decided to throw on a cloak. "Nick? I know it's you."

Nothing. The steps I'd heard stopped. The fear in my stomach *didn't go away, but I used it to keep the ball of fire going. After a few more minutes, the steps started again. They were coming quickly this time.*

The cloaked figure dove at me, almost catching me off guard. I stepped out of the way, pulled off my cloak and threw it over him, making him stumble.

"Why won't you leave me alone? Isn't it enough torture that I have to be here every single night?"

"Because I have no choice," Nick's voice said from beneath the cloaks.

I stared at the pile on the floor, feeling just a small amount of sympathy. Reluctantly, I helped pull the cloaks off him. I needed to understand why he would do this. "What do you mean?"

"I've been sent here to make sure you don't leave. It was easy at first. You ran up and down the stairs for no reason, and I could just sit back and watch." His expression changed to a scowl. "But then you had to ruin it by mixing things up. I was promised riches, but I lost everything when your dad ended up here."

"Well, if you ask me, that was your fault. You left part of your cloak in my room." I folded my arms.

Nick's eyes widened. "Aw, man, she's going to kill me." He jumped up and pushed me against the wall, his hand around my neck. "Did you tell your dad anything about this place?"

I tried to get away, but he was too strong. "Of course I did. He's my dad."

"Yes, but he's awake now. Does he know who I am? How he got here?" His breath stank, and I coughed.

"Yes, he does. I tell him everything." I coughed again. "Seriously, get off me."

He let go and paced the floor. "You may have just killed us both."

"Well, if you hadn't left that piece of cloth behind, my dad would have been off looking for another cure instead of getting stuck here. What did you tear it on, anyway?" I rubbed my neck where he'd pinned me.

"I caught it on your desk when I was messing up your room." He stopped and studied me. "Why does your room look so different from the rest of the house? It's like some kind of mansion, but then your room is full of old, worn-out furniture and faded blankets."

I felt my face redden. "It's just . . . never mind. Stop following me. It's not like I can get out of here anyway." I turned and ran down the stairs, embarrassment keeping me away from him. He had to ask about my family life. If he'd gone to my school, he would know all about my stepsisters and how they treated me. But to have someone from outside realize the difference was like a slap to the face. I was embarrassed that he felt sorry for me.

I came to a landing and pushed at one of the walls to make a room, then ran inside and slammed the door. Broken furniture lay all over the floor. I made another ball of fire and threw it at the wall to let out some frustration. It went out as it hit the stone.

"Temper, temper." A voice came from the doorway.

I whirled to find the woman standing there. Her gown today was long and black. She wore a black hat, and her makeup was dark. "What are you doing here?"

"I must ask you the same thing. You were to stay on the stairs." She raised an eyebrow.

"Yes, well, I wanted a break. Keep your guy off my back. It's bad enough coming here every night. I don't need him pestering me."

"I don't think you're in the position to tell me what to do." She moved inside the room and waved her hand, causing a large chair to appear. "Where is my payment?" Her servants came scurrying inside to bring her food.

Great. I'd made another place for her to hang out. "I already gave it to you."

She laughed. "You think those stones were enough? I suggest you try harder."

I glared. "I don't think you even know what you want." I picked up my skirts and headed for the door. Why my nightgown had suddenly become an old Victorian dress was beyond me.

"If you ever want to leave, you will find it," she called behind me.

I growled and went down a few more landings before allowing myself to rest. I sat on one of the steps and waited to wake up. I really didn't feel like falling down the stairs again to hurry it up.

"Hey, Sydney. Get up!" Julie yelled before throwing something hard on my bed. "You have work to do before this weekend."

I groaned and sat up to find a mop lying across me.

I dropped it on the floor and covered my face with my arm. "We're not doing the party here. It's going to be at the country club."

Julie stiffened. "Plans have already been made to have it here."

"Sorry, but Dad decided last night to do it at the country club." I rubbed my eyes and climbed out of bed.

"That's too bad. We have people ready to come. You will change your plans, or I will make things very miserable for you."

"Fine. But take it up with Dad. Not me." I was too tired to be polite.

She leaned forward until she was only inches from my face. "You will get this changed."

"Syd? Are you rea—" Dad stopped, standing in the doorway. "What's going on?"

Julie backed up. "Sydney was just telling me that she wants to do the party at our house." She hurried over to his side and took his hand.

Dad looked over at me and back at Julie. "You know, I'd like to believe that, but you were right up in her face. What's going on?"

She stared at him before snorting. "We were just having a heart-to-heart. No big deal."

"Look, I don't like how you've been treating my daughter. I'm warning you that I had better not see you talking to her like this again. Do you understand?"

Her eyes blazed. "Fine. I don't have to take this. I'm leaving for now, but I'll be back. I'm your wife, for better or worse." She stormed out of the room.

"I think that was the 'worse' part there." I shuddered.

"Yeah, I think so too." He turned back to me. "Did she threaten you?"

"It's not a big deal, Dad." Okay, so it was. But anything I said against her would come back to bite me. It wasn't worth it.

"Yes, it is. Now, hurry and get dressed. We have some shopping to do." He left the room and closed the door behind him.

He didn't have to tell me twice. I found a nice blouse and some shorts to change into and hurried out to get some breakfast. I wanted to leave before Julie came back.

We went to several stores to pick out napkins and everything else that was needed for a party. We'd decided on navy blue and silver for the colors, and I was amazed at the different fabrics we had to choose from. I kept joking that I felt like I was getting married, but Dad would just smile and tell me he wanted the best for his little girl.

We were done with shopping for the day and stopped for ice cream. We'd looked all over for a dress before deciding on a pink chiffon that went to the floor. Pink wasn't my color, but this one just seemed to work for me.

"So, how did you get off work today?" I asked, savoring a bite of my rocky road shake.

"I told them I had some important work to be done at home. Besides, they need me to go on a business trip for the next couple of weeks, so they let me have today off to make up for it." He stabbed at his ice cream.

"Of course they do." I took another bite, thinking. "Can I come? Please?"

"I'll think about it. I'd like the Order to meet you before you start your senior year."

I bounced in my chair. "Really? That would be so awesome. I'd work hard, I promise. And now that Nick knows . . ." I trailed off, realizing what I'd just said.

He jerked his head up. "Now that Nick knows what? When did you see him?"

"Last night." I explained everything that happened.

"He didn't want me to know who he was?" He raised his eyebrows.

"Yeah, but I don't know why. He didn't tell me. He's not the one who bothers me, though. That woman gives me the creeps. Why did Mom have to go to her?"

Dad took my hand. "Because she wanted a daughter more than anything, Sydney. She would cry herself to sleep every night. You were the answer to her prayer." He cleared his throat and stood. "Let's get going."

I hopped up and followed him out. I loved and missed my mom more than ever after hearing that. I wished I could tell her thank you for what she had done.

We drove over to the country club to drop off the stuff we'd just bought. I felt a jolt when I saw Luke standing in the entrance. There was no way I could face him right then, so I hid in the car while Dad went inside. It hurt to see Luke, knowing he was dating Sarah instead of me, and I wondered if he ever even thought about our time together at camp. The lighthearted mood I'd had while shopping with Dad was gone.

Dad climbed in the car and pulled out of the parking lot. "Luke says hi. And he wants to know if everything's okay."

"Thanks. I'd be fine if he didn't keep going out with my stepsister." I slumped down in my seat.

Dad chuckled. "From what I could see, he isn't thrilled with the situation either."

"Then why are they going out again this weekend?"

"They are? I didn't know. Luke was supposed to be off doing something for the Order, from what his dad was telling me." Dad's phone rang, and he answered it. He mouthed to me that it was Phil and went back to the call.

"Tell him hi," I whispered. He nodded once and kept talking.

We got home to find Julie's car in the driveway, along with a few trucks.

"So much for being gone," I mumbled. I climbed out of the car and went inside to figure out where everyone was. Dad followed behind and went straight to his office.

I walked to the kitchen to look out the back windows. Work crews were totally redesigning the wide expanse of our lawn. What were they doing? Did she really think we would still do the party here? I shook my head and went to my room. When I heard shouting out in the hallway, I stood and crept over to the door.

"I told you we were using the country club. There's no reason to make these changes to the backyard."

"And I told you that we already had things planned for the backyard. Kaylee and Sarah insisted that this is the perfect place to have the party, so that's what we're doing."

"No. I'm sending them all away. This is Sydney's birthday party, and we will do what she wants. If the girls want to have their birthday in our backyard, that is perfectly fine, but this is not their day."

I had rarely heard Dad get this angry. Of course, Dad had spent a lot of money getting his yard just how he wanted it, so Julie was really skating on thin ice with this one.

There was silence on the other side of the door. I'd wondered if they'd walked away, but then I heard the odd, moaning cry Julie liked to use when she didn't get her way. If Dad fell for it again . . .

"Look, I know you're upset, but I'm standing by this.

I need to take off for the rest of the afternoon and tomorrow. I'd better see everything changed back to the way it was when I get home."

I wished I could see what was going on out in the hallway. I sighed and dropped onto my bed. Phil must have thrown this trip on him. It happened often, but I hoped it didn't mean that Dad would miss my party. I stared at the dress Dad bought for me. The only thing that would have been more perfect was if I could dance with Luke while I was wearing it.

I would just have to save those dreams for another day.

Chapter Nineteen

Dad came to my room to say goodbye before he left. He promised that everything would be perfect and he'd be back as soon as he could. What he didn't see were the looks of death I was getting from Julie and her daughters, who were standing behind him.

As soon as he was out of sight, they all turned on me. Julie ordered me to repaint Kaylee's room and give Sarah a manicure. I kept silent, hoping the days would fly so I could get to my party. Unfortunately, time didn't obey, and seemed to drag on forever.

I was also ordered to clean the entire house from top to bottom before I could go to bed. It wasn't how I wanted to spend my night, but at least I wouldn't have to be running from Nick and that woman. I just kept telling myself that all the cleaning was to help my dad, and not because Julie made me do it.

It was past midnight when Julie finally gave up making me use toothpicks to clean out the edges of the stove and around the tile. She sent me to bed with a promise that I would be doing the same thing the next day.

I fell into my bed, not caring about dental hygiene or anything else. I was too emotionally and physically exhausted.

I stood in the center of a staircase that was different from what I'd seen before. It was lighter, happier. But I sensed a sadness, and I couldn't figure out what caused it.

And there were windows. Many, many windows. I walked to the nearest one and saw a large garden that had a maze of shrubs. Fountains and hedges dotted the landscape, and the flowerbeds were filled with roses and tulips and hundreds of other flowers. But where were the people? I ran to the other side of the hall to look out. There was a large driveway full of cars, and a fountain that stood almost as tall as the building I was in. Again, there were no people. What was this place?

I ran down the stairs, holding my skirts high. It was the pink chiffon dress Dad and I had picked out together. I felt like I should be hurrying, but I didn't know why. I stopped on the landing and heard voices below. Not wanting to be seen, I hid behind a nearby column.

A man and woman were speaking in hushed tones, and I tried to get a good look without giving myself away. I leaned forward to see someone who looked a lot like my dad, but he was dressed in a very expensive suit and looked much younger than Dad was now. He was talking to a woman with long dark hair that had streaks of gray running through it. She was dressed in a rich satin dress, and the worry on her face made me want to run to her.

"We must go now," the man said.

"But the girl is just a child. Where will you go?" the woman asked.

"Away. She must not learn of this life. It's too dangerous. I have contacts in other parts of the world. I'll be back when I'm needed."

"You take care of that girl. I plan to see her again one day."

"I will."

The scene faded and I was back on the stairs I saw every night. I sat down on the steps, too shocked to keep moving. What had I just seen? It had to be a random dream, right? But this felt different. Like a memory.

So, if it was a memory, why did my heart ache for that woman? I had wanted to run and put my arms around her. None of it made sense. And was that really my dad?

I stood and walked down the steps, too lost in thought to pay attention to what was going on. My dress had changed, and I was back in the clothes I'd worn to bed.

"It's coming back to you, isn't it?" Nick said from behind me.

I turned around. "You scared me!" I breathed in and out, trying to calm my pounding heart. "What do you mean?"

"You're fading. I think you're closer to getting out of this place than you realize." He sat on the step and pulled his hood back. He looked tired, with rings under his eyes.

"How do I get out?" Desperation flowed through me.

He shrugged. "I don't know, but you seem to be doing a good job of it."

"Did you see that dream?" I stepped closer, feeling a cloak wrap around me. I must have asked for the comfort of it without realizing it.

He shook his head. "I'm stuck in these stairs at night, just like you. I get out when you're awake."

"That doesn't make any sense." I sat down on the landing in front of him.

"Don't you get it? Everything is tied to you. Poor, selfish Sydney has the world revolving around her, and she doesn't even realize it." He sneered.

"Stop. I'm not selfish. You don't even know me." I headed down the stairs again so I could get away from him. He had no idea what I had to put up with every single day. So he had to keep watch over me. Was it that bad?

"You don't have a clue as to what's actually going on here, do you?" Nick asked, catching up to me.

I turned toward him, frustration warring with curiosity. "No, I don't. I'm stuck in this stupid staircase every single night. Up until recently, I couldn't even get rest because I had to run. I don't dream like other people do. If I get hurt here, I'm hurt when I wake up." I stepped closer to him. "All I know is that this is part of some stupid curse that was put on my mom, and when she died, I had to take over for it."

I stormed away. By this time, if I had to fall down the stairs to wake myself up, I was willing to do it.

"Wait."

I kept going so I could stay away from him. I heard him running behind me, and I just sped up. When I couldn't shake him, I stopped on a landing and closed my eyes, thinking of an escape. I pushed on the walls like I'd done at camp. The pain and exhaustion that had hit me at camp was dull here. It was so strange.

I opened my eyes and ran to the door that had formed in front of me. I slammed it as I got inside and froze the door shut. Nick pounded on the door, but I wasn't about to open it.

I studied the room I'd formed. It was a lot like the room I'd made at camp, but this time, the curtains and bedding were a deeper red. Windows lined the walls, and there was a wardrobe in the corner that hadn't been in my room at camp.

A look inside revealed several beautiful gowns. I pulled out a light blue dress and held it up to me. These dresses would all fit me. That made sense, of course, since I was the one who came up with the room.

I touched the ornate brush lying on the dressing table. There was a small mirror with initials carved into it, but they weren't mine. That was weird. I looked around the room to find a nice, plush chair in the corner.

There was another door next to the one where I'd entered. After a moment of hesitation, I decided to try the latch. It opened to a long hallway. Columns lined the walls, and a plush rug ran down the center of a marble floor.

I could either make rooms a lot better now than I had earlier, or I'd transported myself to another place. There was no one around as I walked the halls. It was almost eerie in here. It seemed like there should be people all around, busy with their different jobs, but it stayed empty. Somehow I felt more alone.

I went back the way I came and actually sighed in relief when I found my stairs. I glanced one last time at the room I'd created and closed the door. Nick stood outside, leaning against the doorframe.

"Are you done now? Don't do that again. It makes more work for me." He pushed against the wall, making it disappear.

"So you're here to make sure the stairs stay perfect?" I asked. "Why?"

He shrugged. "I'm supposed to make sure you don't get out."

"Yes, but why? What makes you stay here? Are you in trouble too?"

He glared at me. "That woman is my grandma. I have to do whatever she says. You think I want to be here? I'm stuck until she says so."

"Your grandma? But where are your parents?" I was beginning to see Nick in a different light. I'd never known my grandparents. Dad would change the subject when I asked where they were, so I figured he didn't get along with them.

"*They're home being important people somewhere. I was sent off to be with Grandma when it was revealed that I had magic. I've been watching you ever since.*"

"*I—I'm sorry. Really. But I can't get out of here until I find whatever it is that your grandma wants.*" I stepped forward. "*Do you know what it is?*"

Nick watched me for a minute and almost said something before shaking his head. "*That's something you're going to have to find out for yourself.*"

"*But don't you want to be free of this? I can't get out of here until I find whatever it is. Neither can you.*" I took another step forward, but he started up the stairs.

"*I'm sorry. I can't say anything.*"

I woke up frustrated. I knew he had the answer—I could see it in his face. That meant it was something big, or maybe the punishment would be too harsh if he told me.

I rolled over and glanced at the clock to see that I'd slept in. Julie was going to be ticked if I didn't get her breakfast. But then, since she hadn't actually come to wake me up . . . I rolled over again, closing my eyes. I didn't want to go back to the stairs, but I wasn't ready to climb out of bed yet, either. It was just another couple of days until my party. I wanted it to happen now—being seventeen meant I was only a few months away from getting out of this house. Of course, that also meant leaving Dad in Julie's clutches. I doubted Kaylee or Sarah would go off to college, since homework wasn't something they cared much about.

My stomach growled, and I threw the covers off. Obviously Julie wasn't going to come get me. I climbed out of bed and changed before going over to the door. It was locked. Great. What was the point of locking me in here if they wanted me to be their personal slave?

I pounded on the door. "Hey! Let me out." I pounded again, but no one came. They must have left the house. Or they were outside destroying Dad's yard.

I went over to the window and opened it. There were the same trucks in our driveway that had been there the day before. Yes, she was still up to something. I climbed out the window and went around to the front of the house. I slipped in when a contractor came outside. After grabbing a bowl of cereal, I hid in the bathroom to eat it.

Julie thought it was a punishment for me to be locked in my room. She had no idea that I was actually thrilled to have the day off. I went back out to the kitchen to put my bowl in the sink and looked out the window. The shrubs Dad loved so much were gone—Julie had ordered a stage to be constructed in their place.

My stomach dropped when I saw Sarah in the center

of the yard with her arm through Luke's. He turned just then and looked up at the house. The smile he'd had on his face fell when he caught me staring. He waved, but I just ran back to my room to unlock the door.

I sent a quick text to Dad letting him know what Julie was up to, and then slipped on some shoes and went out to grab my bike. I wasn't about to stick around. My cell phone rang when I'd gone a few blocks from home.

"Hello?"

"Hey, princess. I'll be home in about an hour. I need those people gone—they're not supposed to be near our house."

"What's wrong with them? And I thought you had a business thing." My heart lifted, knowing he would be home soon.

"We got done sooner than we'd thought. And it's just not good for them to be there. They're people I'm worried about."

"Okay. I'll do what I can." Luke was out there. Was there something wrong with him too? I hoped not.

"Oh, and we think we know who the woman is."

I jumped out of my thoughts when I remembered something I'd learned the night before. "It's Nick's grandma," I blurted out. "I found that out last night. She's the one."

There was a pause on the other end. "Are you sure?"

"Yes. He told me himself. He's in charge of making sure I stay there."

"Did you ever get his last name?" Dad asked.

"No. I avoid him as much as possible."

"Right. I want you to find out from Luke, if you can. I know things are weird between you two, but this is very important."

I sighed. "Fine. If I can get him away from Sarah. They seem attached at the hip."

"I still don't think it's what you imagine. Luke has a good head on his shoulders."

"Yeah, I thought so too. See you in an hour." I needed to get off the phone. A couple of neighbors were staring out their windows at me.

"Bye. Love you." Dad ended the call, and I slipped my phone back in my pocket.

I don't think he realized just what he was asking me to do. The trucks were still in the driveway, so I put my bike away and went inside to get a drink of water. Luke was standing in the backyard when I checked through the window, so I texted him a message saying I really needed to talk to him.

He pulled out his phone and then looked up at the window. I ducked down so he wouldn't see me and then peeked back up to see him talking to Sarah, gesturing toward the house. I smiled at the fit she threw.

My heart pounded wildly at the sound of the doorbell. I hadn't talked to him for a while, but my feelings hadn't changed. I cursed my emotions for that reason. After bracing myself and telling my emotions to go away, I opened the door. And melted. I'd forgotten how good he looked this close.

"H—hey, Luke. How's it going?" This needed to be quick. I didn't know how long I had before Sarah would send Julie after me.

He smiled, making my knees weak. Apparently, my emotions hadn't listened. "Hey, Syd. I've missed you. What have you been up to?"

"Oh, nothing. Planning a party, cleaning, riding bikes." Never mind that I'd only gone a couple of blocks. He didn't have to know that.

"Really? I haven't seen you around when I've been here." He blushed. "Look, about Sarah—"

"Just don't. I don't want to hear it." I had to stop the thought before I bawled. "I was just talking to my dad. He's going to be back in about an hour, but he needs to know Nick's last name. Did you ever catch it?"

"Nick? Why?" He thought for a second. "Wait—did you find out more about him?"

"Yes, I've talked to him a few times in my dreams. His grandma has me trapped. Dad wants to find out who she is." Why had I told him so much?

"I never heard his last name, but I'll ask around to see if anyone else knows."

"Thanks." I stood there, not knowing what else to say.

"No problem. And about Sarah . . ." He stopped.

"Oh, there you are. I was beginning to worry." Sarah slipped between us and put her hand on his arm. "What are you doing here?" Her flirtatious smile turned to disgust when she looked at me.

"I live here." I turned around and went to my room. I should have just stayed on my bike ride. I hadn't learned anything else, and I'd had my heart ripped open all over again.

I could hear Luke and Sarah talking out in the hall. I needed something to distract me, so I flopped on my bed and opened my journal to write down everything that had happened. Several minutes later, my door slammed open and Sarah stepped inside my room, eyes blazing.

"What were you doing?" she demanded.

"I have no idea what in the world you're talking about. I was writing in my journal." I pointed down at the book in my hand.

"You don't talk to him. Ever. He's mine." She pointed at herself.

"Whatever. I think he's a big boy and knows what he wants." I wanted to slap her. I wanted to scream and rant and rave, but I just let it slide. When she didn't leave my room, I rolled over and looked at her. "Is there something else?"

"I want you to apologize," she demanded.

I stared at her, incredulous. "Are you kidding me?

Sarah, I just talked to him. Get over yourself and find something else to freak out about." Okay, so I didn't quite let it slide like I'd hoped, but it was better than slapping her.

"What did you talk about?" She folded her arms, still fuming.

"It doesn't matter. Please leave." Dealing with her and everything else was exhausting. I just wanted to take a nap.

She stomped her foot. "I want to know what you talked about. He's *my* boyfriend."

I stood and walked over to the door. "Yes, well, we hung out at camp, and he was quite charming and wonderful to me while we were there. Don't fall for him, or you may regret it. Now get out."

"What do you mean? You think he liked you?" She laughed. "Like that would ever happen." She turned and left, still laughing.

Okay, ouch. He *could* have liked me. Not that it mattered, but I thought we'd been really good friends. And those kisses . . . I shook my head, trying to wipe away the memories. Why did life have to be so hard?

Chapter Twenty

I must have dozed off because the next things I heard were Dad's yelling and Julie's shrieking. I climbed out of bed, still groggy.

I wanted to stay out of it, but figured Dad could use the moral support. It wasn't hard to find them, due to the screaming back and forth. I walked around the corner into the kitchen, and Julie zoomed in on me.

"You! This is your fault."

I raised my eyebrows. "My fault? I was taking a nap."

"The only way your dad could have known about any of this was if you told him."

"You had me locked in my room, remember?" I snapped.

She jerked back and looked between Dad and me. "Of course I didn't."

"Don't give me that, Julie. I know you've done it in the past." He shook his head. "You tell your people to get our yard back the way it was. I have some work to do at the office." He put his arm around Julie before heading out the door. One look at Julie, and I went straight for my room.

"Wait just a minute, Sydney." Julie's voice was like ice.

I turned slowly, knowing this was not going to be pretty. "Yeah?"

"How did you get out of your room?" Her voice was quiet, threatening. That's not what scared me, though. It was the flash I caught in her eyes—a flash I'd never seen before. It made me not only *have* to tell her—it made me *want* to tell her.

"Through my window. That's how I always get out." I clamped my mouth shut before I could tell her that I had magic to unlock doors. How long had she been able to command an answer and get it? Was that why Dad hadn't made her leave yet?

Her smile widened, and she looked almost . . . hungry. "Tell me where your father goes when he leaves town." Again, the flash was there, but I was ready.

"I don't know. Work or something." That was easy enough, since I didn't really know what he was actually doing.

"What does Luke mean to you?" she whispered again.

"He's my protector." I bit my tongue before "boyfriend" came out. That wasn't true, anyway. I backed up, fighting her spell with everything I had.

"What did you do at that camp of yours?" she asked more forcefully.

By this time, I was able to release myself from her grasp enough to think for myself. "We learned pottery." I turned, ran to my room, and slammed the door shut, breathing heavily. Who was this woman? And why had she suddenly shown me this side of herself? I just hoped she didn't know Dad and I had magic or things could get very bad, very quickly.

I heard Julie's door close, so I sat on my bed and texted both my dad and Luke about what had just happened. When that didn't stop me from shaking, I decided to text Jade and the other girls as well and asked if any of them had heard Nick's last name.

The girls didn't know anything about Nick, but they did agree that something bad was going on. Jade offered to come over and get me out of harm's way, and Heidi asked if we should go bowling. I told them both I was okay and didn't want to put them in the middle of it.

I was replying to Katy's suggestion of toilet papering the house when my phone rang. It was a number I recognized, but I wasn't sure why.

"Hello?"

"This is Phil. Your father didn't turn up at the office

like he'd said, so I went after him. He's been in an accident." Phil's voice sounded solemn, and my heart plummeted.

"Is he okay?" I could barely get my mouth to form the words.

"He's unconscious. The doctors say he'll pull through, but he's in the hospital so they can keep an eye on him."

Hot tears ran down my cheeks. "But my party is tomorrow." I grimaced, realizing how that sounded, but my brain couldn't concentrate on what was going on. Dad had just returned from his deep sleep, and now he was gone again.

"We know. We have our best healers working on him. Listen, though. You can't let your stepmother know what's going on. There's a chance she was involved."

"Wh—what do you mean?" I knew she was capable of it, but it still felt like a knife to my heart.

"From what we can tell, one of her gardeners ran him off the road. My driver saw one of their trucks fleeing the scene when we got there. Sydney, listen to me. You need to go along with everything she says. You can't let her know anything is wrong. Do you understand?"

"But what about my dad?" I whispered. I could hear Julie outside my door, talking to Kaylee or Sarah.

"This is the only way to keep both of you safe. Also, keep trying to get Nick's last name. Your father's life may depend on it." The phone went dead.

Just then, a few texts came through. Luke still hadn't had any luck, but my stomach jumped when I saw the text from Liz.

Hey, I talked to Max. He said Nick's last name is something like Naraka. Hope that helps.

I texted back a thank you and sent the name off to Luke. Then I paced the floor, trying to figure out what to do next. When Julie pounded on the door and demanded that I come and clean, I welcomed the distraction.

The list she'd given me was very long, and it would take until midnight or longer to get it done. The cleaning, laundry, dishes, and making beds were okay. Having to fix what Julie's crew had done was ridiculous. She could have easily called them back to take apart the stage and replant the shrubs that had been ripped out.

After a call to our regular nursery, I started working on the stage. The sun was hot on my back, but I wasn't about to go inside to get something to drink. The head gardener from the nursery showed up with the plants I'd ordered. I thanked him and waved before turning back to my task.

When my arms were sore from pulling out nails, I stopped to take a break. I heard someone approaching and turned to see who it was.

"I thought you could use a drink." Luke handed me a glass of juice and pulled out some work gloves.

"Thank you." I drank the juice without taking a breath.

"It's got to be over a hundred degrees out here." He glanced around. "So what are we working on?"

I blinked. "We?"

"Yes. I'm not letting you do this all on your own. Besides, I need to talk to you about Nick."

Oh. Right. "Well, we're planting the shrubs where the others used to be, and this stage needs to be taken down."

"Got it. And we're doing this why?" He took a hammer and started on the stage.

"Because Julie put it up without asking Dad first." I grabbed a shovel and started on the first shrub. I pushed away thoughts of my dad lying in a hospital bed—I didn't want to cry in front of Luke.

"Right, but why are you the one doing it?" He pulled off the board and threw it on the pile.

"Because that's what I do." I smiled and kept digging.

"You're kidding, right?"

"No. Now what did you want to say about Nick?" I bent down to pull out the roots from the old shrub.

"You don't recognize that last name?"

"Should I?" I set the new plant inside to see if it would fit. The hole was still too shallow, so I took it out to keep digging.

"If you'd grown up taking the same history classes I did, you would. It's a very old wizard family name. Some wizards do a lot of good for the magic world. Others, like Nick's grandma, are evil to the core. Your mom must have been desperate to go to her."

I wasn't too surprised that Lady Naraka was evil. After all, she'd had me running those stairs for years. But if I stopped her, what would happen to Nick? "So, do we know how to defeat her?"

Luke turned from the stage. "No. We're researching to find her weaknesses, but from what we've found, she has none. Only a few people know where she is and it sounds like you're one of them, along with Nick."

"Dad thinks she lives on the stairs." I looked over at Luke.

"That's what my dad thinks too. Otherwise, you and Nick wouldn't be able to get in so easily. *We* just don't know how to get there."

I finished with the shrub and moved on to the next one. "So let me guess. I have to be the one to stop her."

Luke nodded. "Yes. Sorry. I wish I could help you, but it's your dream, so that's where it has to stop."

"Of course." I pulled out the roots to the old shrub and dug out enough dirt to plant the next one.

"Okay, the stage is pretty much done. I want to stay and help you, but Dad doesn't want Sarah or anyone else to catch me with you. It could cause big problems."

"It's fine. I'll do the rest. Thanks for your help." I picked up the next shrub. "Luke, can you do me a favor? Will you check on my dad? I want to go visit, and it's killing me that I can't."

He put his arm around me and squeezed before letting go. "Of course. I'm sorry for what happened. We'll stop whoever is doing this."

I met his eyes. "You know Julie's part of it, right?"

He glanced up at the house. "Yes. We're just trying to figure out how she's connected to everything. Be careful." He waved and walked away.

That was easy for him to say—he wasn't the one living with Julie. I finished up the shrubs and then continued pulling apart the frame of the stage. The sun had set by the time the boards were all in a pile and the nails were in the garbage. I'd call for one of my dad's landscapers to come pick up the boards in the morning.

I headed up to the house and climbed the stairs to the back porch, but found Julie standing there with her arms folded. When I tried to get around her, she stepped in front of me again.

"Can you please move? I'm tired and I want to go to bed. I've been working outside all day."

"Your job isn't done." She smiled widely, making me shiver.

"The sun is down. You really can't expect me to keep working, can you?"

Her smile only got wider. "Oh, but I can. We have lights out there. You won't come in this house until you've finished your job."

My jaw dropped. "You have got to be kidding me." I grumbled and went into the garage to get a wagon for the boards. By the time I was finished loading them up and putting them by the driveway, it was past midnight. Sometimes it was seriously annoying to have such a large yard.

When I was satisfied that the yard was just like it had been before—except for the holes where the posts had been put in for the stage—I trudged back up to the house and into my bedroom. I grabbed my clothes and heard a click from the other side—she'd just locked me in again. I groaned inwardly. So much for a shower. I could have just gone through the window again, but Phil had warned me not to ruffle any feathers.

I flopped onto my bed and willed sleep to come. If I knew my stepmom, she would have plenty for me to do tomorrow.

I refused to run the stairs. I had been a slave to Julie since she moved in and Dad went off on his business trips, and I was sure she'd never worked me as hard as she had that day. True, the magic had worn me far past this, but it was a different kind of exhaustion.

I imagined myself a pillow and blanket and made myself comfortable in the corner of the landing. I had almost dozed off when I saw a pair of combat boots right in front of me.

"You're breaking the rules, you know." Nick looked down at me, arms folded.

"I don't care." I turned so I could look up at him better.

"You will if my grandma gets a hold of you. You're supposed to be paying this thing off." He leaned against the wall.

"Could you sit down so I don't have to look up at you? It's hurting my neck," I said.

He grunted and sat, crossing his legs. "You've done this for years and never had a problem with it. Why are you breaking rules all of a sudden?"

"I didn't know I had a choice. Besides, my dreams started changing a few weeks ago—I don't know why. Then I realized I could play with them." I sat up. "I want out, Nick. I don't want to be here anymore. I can't imagine you do, either."

Nick watched me for a minute before looking down at his hands. "No. I'm tired."

"Where do you go when you're awake?" I had learned his last name, but I didn't know anything else about him.

"I just kinda live wherever I can find a place. My mom disappeared a while after I was sent to watch over you."

I tried to push away my sympathy for him. He'd been my captor. My guard. He'd been rude to me and the other campers. But if he'd had all his freedom taken from him, did he have much of a choice? Well, of course he did. I wasn't exactly free to do what I wanted and I was nice . . . wasn't I? Thoughts flickered past, making me want to invite him to my party, but I ignored them. I had enough of him at night.

He stood up. "You really should get going."

"Why don't you just stay here and make sure I don't leave? Then you'd be doing your job, right?" I asked.

"Er, not really. You're supposed to be running. But I guess as long as I know where you are . . ."

"Right. Just don't let your grandma or anyone else near me." I rolled over and closed my eyes, hoping the rest I got here would help when I woke up in the morning.

I had nearly fallen asleep when I heard Nick swear under his breath, followed by approaching footsteps.

I scrambled to stand and ran away from whoever was coming. When I had gone up a few stories, I stopped to listen. I could hear Nick talking with his grandma. Emotions warred inside me. I wanted to get far away from her, but I was dying to hear what they were saying.

Curiosity won out and I crept down to where I could hear them better, but they still couldn't see me. I closed my eyes and strained to listen, bracing myself in case I had to start running again.

"She failed to get the stage set up for the full moon. Cinderella's father was able to resist her magic this time. This will hinder our plans, but it is no matter. We can still make it happen."

"What do you mean?" Nick's voice echoed off the walls.

"Now that her father is out of the picture, things can happen more quickly. At the stroke of midnight, she will be stuck here

forever, never to be freed. The only way to break the curse is to be kissed as the bell tolls, and Sarah has taken care of that." Her menacing laugh made me shiver. *I couldn't be stuck here! I leaned forward.*

"But . . . why?" he asked.

"I need her magic, and I can't have it unless she remains alive. Her magic possesses an imprint I need, but I cannot have it if she is dead. Trapping her here will keep her alive forever."

I gasped. Luke was right—I had to destroy this place. But how was I supposed to do that? I'd made small things happen. This was tearing down walls. And if I pulled the staircase down, I could go with it. Of course, if I didn't stop her, my life would essentially be over anyway.

I turned and ran up the stairs, trying to clear my head. Listening was dangerous when Nick's grandma was on the loose, especially if she knew I had the answer to getting out of here. I needed Luke's help, but would he kiss me? Maybe. He had before. I blushed at the thought of his lips on mine. There was a huge problem with this plan—he was Sarah's date. Messing with her was not something I wanted to do, but I didn't see any way around it.

Chapter Twenty-One

I woke the next morning, my mind a jumble of thoughts about what I would have to do to free myself. I'd been looking forward to this day for a very long time. It was my birthday, and yet I didn't feel like celebrating. There was too much to get done, so instead of being excited for a new year, there was a weight on my shoulders.

Except that I had a glimmer of hope. I could make this happen if I did it just right. I grabbed my phone off my lamp table and texted Luke a little of what I'd learned last night. I kept the kiss from him because I didn't want him acting different around Sarah at the ball—it could mess things up. Instead, I just told him I would need his help and left it at that.

I then texted Phil to see if my dad was okay. It was

agony waiting to get answers back, but I was relieved when I did. Luke promised to do whatever was needed, and Phil let me know that Dad was out of his coma and demanding to go home to his little girl. The healers who had come during the night had apparently done a great job with him.

I climbed out of bed, hoping for a hot shower before starting the day, but the door was still locked. When I tried the window, it was stuck. The metal almost looked like it had been melted shut. Someone in this house *did* have powers Dad hadn't known about. I went back to the door and pounded on it.

A key turned in the lock, but it was only to allow Sarah to shove a bowl of cereal at me. Before I could ask anything, she'd slammed the door again and locked it. I sat down on my bed to eat, trying to figure out a way to escape. Using my magic on the doorknob would only work if I knew for sure they were out of the house. I didn't want any of them to know I had magic too.

By the time they let me out of my room, I'd painted my nails, planned out the night, read a book, and color-coordinated everything in my closet. A glance at the clock told me we only had a couple of hours until the dance, and I still needed a shower.

"Sydney, I want my hair up in a bun, with curls around it." Sarah sat down in front of the mirror in the bathroom.

"But I still need to get ready."

She glared. "Mom! Sydney's not helping me!"

Julie poked her head out of her bedroom. Her hair was up in curlers and she was wearing a face mask. "Sydney, get Sarah's hair done. Now."

"But—" I stopped at the look on her face and growled. "Fine. I'll do this, but then I'm going to get ready." I pulled her hair up and put clips all over in it to keep anything from falling out. The curls were done quickly, and I turned to go.

"Uh-uh. You haven't done my hair yet." Kaylee popped her gum and sat down next to Sarah. "I need mine straightened. It makes me look taller."

I raised an eyebrow and chose to say nothing. Her hair was soon straight and smooth. I added a diamond-encrusted clip and then stepped back. "Okay, *now* can I go?"

Sarah studied Kaylee's hair for a second. "No, I think I want what she has instead. I really do need to look a little taller for Luke's sake." The batting of her eyelashes sent my annoyance through the roof.

"Your hair is fine how it is. And whoever said that straight hair makes you taller?"

Sarah reached up and pulled the pins out of her hair. "I want what Kaylee has—now. Or I'll show all your embarrassing pictures to Luke."

I didn't have a clue what pictures she was talking

about, but I didn't want to find out. "All right. Straight it is." Once I was done, I turned to leave, but Kaylee grabbed my arm.

"Where do you think you're going? I'm not about to go to the ball looking like Sarah. I want my hair up."

"If I do it, will you two promise you'll let me get ready after that?"

"Fine. I have to go get dressed anyway." Sarah stood and went to her room.

"Whatever." Kaylee filed her nails while I pulled her hair up and did it the same way I'd done Sarah's just minutes before. She popped her gum and went to her room without thanking me.

While they argued over necklaces and what to wear, I jumped into the shower. Once I was done, I hurried past their room to change. I was so excited about how the pink dress looked on me. I readjusted the bow on the waistline until it looked right. Now I just needed to get my hair dried and pulled back with bobby pins, so I left my room to find the blow dryer.

Kaylee stopped putting on mascara and dropped the wand. "Where did you get that? It's gorge—hideous. I can't believe you'd wear that anywhere."

"Yeah, it's terrible. I mean, look at that bow." Sarah sneered and reached forward, pulling it off.

I gasped. "What did you do that for?" I stared down in horror at the gaping hole she'd left behind.

"She had good reason. It was awful. And the lace on the bodice? Ick. So last year." Kaylee laughed as she ripped off the lace, taking a layer of taffeta with it.

"And you'd better watch your step. You wouldn't want the skirt to tear." Sarah grabbed and yanked, filling the air with a loud rip.

Tears poured down my face as they continued to pull my dress to bits. When Julie came out to see what was going on, she simply sniffed and walked into the kitchen. I ran for my room, my dress in pieces. I sobbed as I heard the girls get picked up by their dates. They were loud and giggly just outside my door. Julie left soon after, with a laugh that chilled me. They had been cruel before, but nothing compared to what they had just done.

I pulled off the remains of my dress and put on my robe until I could figure out something else to wear. My phone buzzed, and I picked it up to see that Jade had texted me. I wiped my eyes so I could see the words through my tears.

Hey, we got here early. Coming?
I let out a sob and typed the reply.
Not sure if I'm going to make it. Stepsisters ruined my dress.

Suddenly I was receiving angry texts from the other girls, demanding to know what was going on. They wanted to come over and save me, but I wasn't about to let them ruin their dates.

Remembering what I'd done with the blue dress before, I went to my closet to find a dress to work on. The dress they'd torn to shreds was so bad, there wasn't anything I could do with it except throw it out, so I had to using something else. My dresses were gone—every one of them. But how did they get in? I checked the lock that Dad had changed, only to find that it had been broken. Someone in the house really didn't want me to look good for my own ball. I tried to make a dress out of a couple of my shirts, but they were way shorter than I would ever wear. I sat down on my bed in defeat. There was the robe I was wearing, but I didn't know if I could make it work.

The knock at my bedroom door made me jump. Everyone should have been at the dance. I froze, not knowing what to do.

The knock came again. "Sydney? Open up, princess."

Dad! I ran over and threw open the door. "What are you doing home?" I stopped, seeing his black eye and the cut on his forehead. "Oh, Daddy. What did they do to you?"

"I'm fine. Just don't hug me or you might hurt my ribs." He smiled. "You didn't think I'd miss my girl's birthday, did you?"

"Well . . ." I laughed, but then started crying. "I can't go to my own party, Dad. They ruined my dress." I pointed over at the mess that was once my gown.

"Wow, they really did a number on it, didn't they?" He chuckled. "Good thing I'm here to save the day." He nodded at the entryway, and Phil stepped inside holding a blue gown that made it hard for me to breathe. The dress from my dreams. "What do you think?" he asked.

"It's beautiful." I couldn't move to take it from Phil. I didn't want to wear it, but Dad looked so happy with himself, I didn't have the heart to tell him this dress brought back nightmares.

"Go ahead, sweetie. Try it on." He took the dress and handed it to me, beaming.

I smiled weakly and closed the door. What was I supposed to do? I could change the color or the style, but it would give away the fact that I didn't like it. I finally pulled it on and zipped it up. It felt like it was made for me. It fit every curve and flared out where it should. I felt just like the princess my dad had always insisted I was. I opened the door, and my dad stared for a second before pulling me into a hug. I was careful when I wrapped my arms around him, but still heard a sharp intake of breath. "Oh, sorry."

"When did you grow up to be such a beautiful young woman?" he asked, wiping his eyes.

"Oh, stop." I hurried over to the mirror to figure out what to do with my hair. I needed something more than what I'd been planning.

Phil stepped forward and gestured for me to sit.

"Allow me." He pulled my hair up and into a twist in the back of my head.

"Where did you learn to do that?" I asked.

"I have a few daughters of my own. I had to learn quickly." He winked and stepped aside.

Dad came forward. "Don't forget the accessories. Every girl needs a tiara." He set a delicate tiara with crystals on my head and nestled it among my dark curls. He also handed me some gloves and a mask. "Let's surprise everyone at the party." He held out his arm. "Are you ready?"

The girl looking back at me was happy and content. "I've never been more ready."

"Then you'll need these." He held out a pair of glass heels. They reflected in the light, sending rainbows everywhere.

"They're gorgeous. But how am I supposed to dance or even walk in these?"

"Just try them. They were your mom's. I've been saving them for the perfect moment."

I took them, afraid I would drop one and shatter it. They fit perfectly and were surprisingly comfortable. "Thank you. Let's go."

"Your carriage awaits, m'lady." He gestured toward the door with a bow. It was only slightly marred by his gasp of pain.

I took the mask and gloves from Dad and walked

beside him out to the limo he must have ordered for the night—his car had been totaled, after all.

On the drive to the country club, Dad told me what had happened. He'd left for the office and noticed about halfway there that a car was following him and coming up fast. He tried to move out of the way, but the car managed to knock him off the road. He didn't remember anything after that.

"What are we going to do about Julie?" I asked, trying to control the anger coursing through me.

"We don't have a lot of proof yet that it was her. We'll just have to keep things quiet until we can do something."

"But you'll get hurt again," I argued.

"I have faith that you'll have it taken care of long before I need to worry about that." He patted my knee. "Ah, we're here. Now keep that mask on. I don't want Julie knowing where you are."

"Won't it look strange, me being the only one with a mask?"

He looked at me in surprise. "Didn't you know it would be a masquerade? We're all wearing them, which is great since that means I can hide this black eye of mine."

Phil helped Dad out of the car and then took my hand. He bowed slightly. "Knock 'em dead." Phil then spoke into a walkie-talkie, and four men came over and stood on each side of Dad. Apparently they weren't taking any chances.

I took a deep breath. I could do this. It was just a simple dance, after all. Dad took my arm and we headed into the country club together. The music blasted as we walked toward the ballroom.

We came down the stairs, and the room seemed to hush. Okay, so it didn't really—but it would have added to our dramatic entrance. Dad was right—there were masks everywhere. I relaxed and nodded to him before walking around, trying to find my friends.

I noticed a group of five girls giggling and talking to each other while their dates stood around, looking uncomfortable. That was them, all right.

"Hey," I said as I walked up.

Jade squealed from behind her peacock mask. Her dress was royal blue with green swirls that matched her mask perfectly. "You made it. We were about to send out a rescue team."

"My dad came to save me."

"He did? Julie announced that he was in the hospital." Heidi was wearing a cat mask to accent her sleek black dress. Blake couldn't seem to keep his eyes off her.

"Yes, well, he's doing much better than my stepmom hoped." I filled them on everything that had happened.

Katy shook her head. "That's just plain wrong. So what are you going to do?"

"I'm supposed to kiss someone at midnight." I tried to find Luke, but it was impossible in this place. Everyone was dancing and moving.

"Luke's over there. We've been keeping an eye on him." Ashley gestured toward the dais at the back of the ballroom.

"And of course Sarah's not going to let go of him," I mumbled.

"Oh, that's easy. At every slow song, she yanks him onto the floor. You'll just have to cut in." Jade pointed up at the speaker as it began to broadcast a slow love song and then nodded over at Luke.

Sarah jumped up and pulled Luke along with her. He watched everyone around them as he walked past. When he came by me, he stopped and said something to Sarah. She put her hands on her hips and argued, but he gestured toward the restroom. Sarah finally stomped back to her seat. Luke waited a second and then made his way over to me.

"You're here." His voice sent warm tingles through my body. His wolf mask hid his dimples, but I would know those eyes anywhere.

"Yes, I am. How's the party?" I had no idea what I was supposed to be doing. My knees had gone weak and my mouth had gone dry.

"It's much better now that you're here. Would you care to dance?" He held his hand out to me.

I placed my hand in his and met his eyes, heart pounding. "Of course." I floated out to the dance floor and melted when he put his arms around me. The shoes I'd been so worried about seemed to know what they were doing and allowed me to glide along with him.

"What took you so long to get here? I was really worried when you didn't come with us to the ball," he whispered in my ear.

"I had to wait for my fairy godmother. Or, really, my dad." I giggled, picturing him with wings and a fairy wand.

"He's here?" Luke stiffened. "I'm glad he's okay, but he could be in big trouble here. When did he get out of the hospital?"

"I don't know, but he showed up at our house and brought me a dress."

"How did he know you needed one?" he asked.

I shrugged. "Phil told me we're watched all the time. I figured they saw the girls ripping my other dress to shreds."

"Well, he did a great job picking it out. You look beautiful." Luke pulled me in closer.

"Thank you." I could feel my face burn at hearing him say that. "I didn't have the heart to tell him that I've worn this dress in my dreams."

"Well, let's hope we can stop those nightmares. Do you have any idea how you're going to stop Lady Naraka? I'm really worried about your dad."

"I am too, but he insisted on coming. He has four guards surrounding him, so we'll just have to trust him." I was glad Luke couldn't see my face at that point. How was I supposed to tell him that I knew exactly how I was going to stop her, and it included kissing him? I took a deep breath, bracing myself. "I know what to do."

"You do? That's great!" His smile helped me continue with what I had to say.

"You need to know something." I told him all about what I'd learned in the dream. While I was glad for *my* mask, I wished I could see his face to know how he felt about it.

"Well, I guess we'll just have to make it a kiss to remember." He laughed and changed our slow dance to a waltz.

The rest of the room faded. I laid my head on his chest, happy to be with him again.

After the song ended, Luke pulled away from me. "I'm so sorry, but I really need to go be with Sarah. Otherwise, your stepmom will be suspicious." He nodded toward the dais where Sarah sat, her arms folded, looking bored. Julie was standing, watching the crowd with her hands on her hips.

I felt like I'd had a bucket of water thrown over me.

"Oh. Right. You go. I'll be with my friends." I turned, but he grabbed my arm.

"Look, I would love to spend every second with you. It's killing me to walk away. I'll be back as soon as I can— I promise." He hurried toward where Sarah sat, glancing over his shoulder at me.

I walked through the crowd to find my dad, and suddenly the feeling of being watched was strong. Someone was here. Nick? I twisted in circles, trying to find him, but the masks kept everyone's faces hidden.

I spotted my dad near the back of the room. It was hard to mistake his tall build. I hurried over to him.

"Dad, someone's here who shouldn't be." I was shaking with fear. I wasn't ready to stand up to Lady Naraka yet, but if Nick was here, I was running out of time.

"What? Here? How do you know?" He stood up straight and sent his guards around.

"I feel him watching me."

Dad glanced up at the large clock on the wall. "We have a while before midnight. Go try to blend in. Don't go near your friends, because Nick knows who they are. Find someone else to chat with. I'll keep an eye on you."

"Okay." I weaved my way through to the opposite of the room and stood there, pretending to be part of the group but keeping watch around me. I danced a few times with different guys and always kept my answers vague. Yes, I was from around here. No, I didn't know where Sydney was. I would give them my phone number later.

I was pretty sure I'd eaten half the banquet table during fast songs. Dad had only taught me the waltz and the foxtrot, and I wasn't about to try something that would bring attention to myself. I was relieved when there were only a few minutes left until midnight. I looked over to find Luke, but he wasn't on the dais with Sarah. My stomach plummeted.

"May I have your attention, please?" Julie stood at the top of the stairs. "It's that time you've all been waiting for. We'll pull off our masks so everyone knows who they've been talking to and dancing with all evening." She let out a fake laugh and continued. "At the count of ten." She began counting, and I panicked. They weren't supposed to take off the masks until midnight. I couldn't let Julie find me.

Everyone pulled off their masks, and the ballroom was filled with talking as everyone met up with friends they'd been looking for. I slowly pulled off my mask, hoping to find Luke before it was too late.

The clock was almost to midnight when I saw Luke standing near the stairs. I pushed my way through the crowd, apologizing as I went. I couldn't see Sarah or Kaylee, so I needed make my move while I could.

I came up right behind Luke, whispering his name. He turned and grinned before pulling me close.

"Now, about that kiss." He leaned down and kissed me softly, adding more pressure and passion.

Suddenly he was yanked away, leaving me standing there, breathless. Sarah held on to his arm, fire in her eyes.

"How dare you? He's mine!" she spat at me.

Kaylee and Julie grabbed my arms, their fingernails digging into my skin. Julie leaned forward. "You just thought you could get away with this. We see you for who you really are."

Just then, the clock struck midnight, and I stared at Luke in horror. It was too late. I tried to use my magic to get away, but somehow I couldn't summon it. But anger built up inside me, and I was able to rip my hands out of their grasp.

"No, Julie. I see you for who *you* are. Get away from my dad. Get away from my house. And make sure I never see you again." I punched her as hard as I could in the face before running for the stairs. I was pretty sure I'd broken something in my hand, but man, it felt good to hit her.

And then time slowed. Everyone drifted away and I was in my dream, living my nightmare. I was wearing the same dress, but somewhere along the way, I had lost one of my shoes. They were terrible to run stairs in, but I couldn't help the tear that fell. It was one more thing from my mom that I'd lost. I forced myself to concentrate on what was happening. If I could believe Nick's grandma, I was stuck here forever, and I was really not okay with that. I needed to get out of here, and soon.

I picked up my skirts and began running, hoping for some kind of break in this nightmare. I sobbed and looked around, trying to find anything besides the stairs. There had to be some way.

I created door after door on each landing, but they were all locked. I pounded on one, screaming at the top of my lungs. I needed to get back and save my dad. Something was going to happen to him, and I couldn't stop it. I slid down the wall, not caring that my dress was now dirty. I had never wanted to wear this one anyway.

Nick came up the stairs to where I sat. "You failed. I knew you would. You're not strong enough." He laughed and sat next to me.

"Why are you doing this? Don't you want out of here too?" I yelled. Surely the guy had some sense of decency in him.

Nick laughed again, cruelly this time. "You have no clue what you're up against. This place? This is my home. I don't want to leave. Why would I ever help you?" He stood and began to walk away.

I felt like I'd been slapped. "You've been lying to me? You really are a complete jerk, aren't you?"

He bowed. "Of course I am. It runs in my blood, but you should know that by now. You did enough snooping around to find out my last name. I just had to slip it into Max's memory."

"That makes no sense. Why did you want me to know?" My head spun. I'd lost everything, and he was just rubbing it in.

"Fear, Syd. Fear. Everyone knows my family means business. I wanted you to give up. This tower, my grandma—even my mom feeds off fear. And you have plenty of it."

I cracked. I was sick of being bullied, and I wasn't about to let him do the same thing to me. I thought of a prison. I imagined the slimy walls, the brick, the iron bars, and even the rats, and then I pushed it as hard as I could at Nick.

The room appeared and hit Nick with full force, knocking him back. He smacked the wall and slid down, not moving. I hoped he would be okay, but that wasn't what I needed to worry about right now. I had to find his grandma and make this stop. I ripped off the lace from the bottom of my dress and tied up his hands and feet to make sure he couldn't get away when he woke up.

I ran to the stairs, yelling to get the woman's attention. Fear coursed through my veins, and I couldn't get away from it—fear that Julie had managed to find my dad, and fear that I would lose.

But . . . why? Why did I need to fear? I looked down at my hands. I had done pretty amazing things with these hands over the last little bit, and I knew that I had more power and energy than ever before. I had my dad. I had friends who really cared about me. And I had Luke. It was time to stop fearing.

It was then that I felt someone nearby. Someone I hadn't sensed in the tower before. I heard crying from behind me. It wasn't Nick, because he was still out cold against the wall. I turned and ran toward the sobs. Somehow, they were familiar to me.

I came to a cell that was old and rusted. The solid walls were made of steel, and it was dark inside.

"Hello?" I called.

The crying stopped. "Hello?" The voice was weak, but it sent a shock through me. It was a voice I never thought I'd hear again.

"M—Mom?" I called.

There was silence. "Sydney?"

I let out a sob. "Mom! I thought you were dead." I looked around for something to unlock the door with and then shook my head. I had magic. "Mom, scoot back." I used fire to weaken the door, and then ice to harden and shatter it.

I ran inside and over to the woman I'd missed more than anything in my life. I pulled her into my arms and we sobbed together. Mom was thin, and I felt like I was going to break her, but I had her in my arms. Joy filled my soul, and I knew what I had to do.

I closed my eyes and thought of the most beautiful place I could imagine—the castle. I pushed hard while holding tightly to my mom.

I heard a shriek as I burst through one of the walls of the stairwell. The woman was nearby. I quickly opened the door to the castle and set Mom inside. "You stay here. I'll be back—I promise." I closed the door and sealed it before turning to face the evil sorceress, Lady Naraka.

"So, you think you can defeat me?" She moved forward, holding her side. Her skin was paler than usual.

"I know I can." I stood strong, my hands clenched into fists.

"Mighty words for such a weak mage," she sneered. Her breaths were ragged as she gasped for air. What had happened to her? She'd been fine the last time I saw her.

"I'm twice the mage you ever were. Besides, I have my mom, and if you hadn't noticed, your grandson is unconscious. It's you and me." We circled each other, and I watched for her to make a move.

She glared. "Very well." She lifted her hand and used her magic to throw me against the wall.

I rolled over and groaned. The shield I'd been preparing disintegrated—I needed to move faster. This wasn't just practice with Luke anymore. Pushing up, I concentrated on the air around me. I faced her smugness and gritted my teeth. She did have strong magic. I would have to figure out a way to get around it.

"I believe it's your move." She continued to hold her side, but stood straighter.

"Okay." As much as I hated her, as much as I wanted to hurt her, I couldn't. I was raised better than that. But what I could do was destroy the very place where I'd been held prisoner. Instead of attacking her, I used wind to push against the stones, knocking a few out of the walls.

She dropped to the ground, shrieking, and I stood there in surprise. It seemed that every time I destroyed part of the walls, it hurt the sorceress. After a few seconds, she was able to stand back up. "Stop doing that." She flung out her hand and threw her magic at me again.

My head slammed against the wall, and my vision doubled for a moment. I pushed away, forming a fireball in my hand, but she slapped me with a rope of ice that sliced my cheek. Another blow hit me in the stomach, making me bend over, the wind knocked out of me. Blow after blow came, not allowing me to do anything but curl up and wait for it to stop.

She paused for a moment to catch her breath, and I took the chance to think of my options. Attacking her would only give her the chance to come after me. But if I destroyed the tower, it would hopefully defeat her too. There was only one way to find out. I put my hand on the wall and pushed, making the rocks turn to ice. Then

I concentrated on the mortar holding the rocks together, and then used fire and wind to blow out again. This time, a large chunk of the wall was torn away, along with some of the floor.

Lady Naraka fell forward, gasping. Her sleek hair was beginning to gray and fall out. She reached out again, but this time, I easily pushed her magic away. She was weakening. I sent out another blast of fire and wind, knocking out more walls. The ceiling above us began to tip, and I pushed against it with everything I had to make it fall away from us. There was no reason to get smushed while I attempted to save the day—I just hoped there was no one below when it landed.

I walked to the woman and bent down. "You may have had power over my mother and many other innocent people, but today, you will be repaid for all the damage you've done."

Laughter filled the room. "Little Sydney has developed a backbone, I see."

I turned to see Julie standing there in her ball gown. Her nose was swollen from when I'd punched her, but her smug look remained.

"What are you doing here?" I'd known she was involved somehow, but it was still a shock to see her here.

"Oh, didn't you know? This is my dear old mommy." She sneered down at the woman lying on the floor.

"But . . . that means . . ."

Julie made a clucking noise. "You're very slow today, aren't you?" She pointed over at Nick, who still hadn't moved. "That's my son you knocked out."

I rubbed my head, trying to make sense of everything. "You had a son and you made him stay here? Why didn't you have him come live with us?"

Julie laughed. "He was useless to me there. I sent him to live with *her* so she could teach him magic. Obviously, it didn't work."

"So you were helping your mom get my magic?" All the chores, all the horrible things she'd said. But even that didn't add up.

Julie laughed. "Oh, dear child. This was never about my mother. She was just the means to getting what *I* wanted." She made a fireball with both her hands and shot it toward Lady Naraka, blowing her off the edge of the tower. "And now, to finish this. You have something I n—" She fell forward as the tower began to buckle. "What's happening?"

It was my turn to laugh. "You just destroyed the only thing keeping this tower together. Without your mom, it's going to fall. Goodbye, Julie." I wrapped myself in wind and water and pushed down as hard as I could, destroying the tower below me. I used the rest of the energy I had to transport myself to the castle just as the darkness closed over me.

I tried to make sense of the dreams I'd had, but they were a jumble of memories. Home, a boy, glass slippers. I wanted to rub my face, but my arms were too sore.

"Look! She's waking up," a voice said above me.

"Jade, leave her alone. She's exhausted," Liz's voice said off to the side.

Wait—what? My eyes flew open, and I jolted upright. I was in a hospital room, and my friends were sitting around me.

"The dreams. They're gone!" I exclaimed, then grabbed my head and groaned. Okay, sitting up fast was a bad idea.

"Whoa, slow down, Syd. You're going to pass out again." Jade put her hand on my shoulder and helped me lay back on the bed. "You gave us all a shock when you disappeared, and the next thing we know, you're in the hospital. Now, please rest."

"But you don't understand. I had a dream with no stairs." My heart was full and I was happy. I looked away from the girls and saw a woman lying in the bed next to mine.

"Hey, sweetie," Mom said weakly.

My eyes filled with tears. Mom. "So that wasn't just a dream? You're really here?" Flashes of a battle flew through my head, but I pushed them away. They only made my head hurt worse.

"I'm really here." She coughed, and the nurses hurried over to her side.

"Where are we?" I should have been in a castle somewhere.

"You're close to home. Your dad's outside." Jade grinned. "Luke's been calling every few minutes to find out how you're doing."

"I'm home?" Relief washed over me. "Wait—what happened to Sarah and Kaylee?"

The girls glanced at each other before Jade turned to me. "We kinda accidentally turned them into statues."

"*What?*" My jaw dropped. "How did that happen?"

Katy grinned. "We all attacked at once when you disappeared. Each of our spells interacted with the shield Kaylee tried to produce, and it exploded on the two of them. It's too bad we didn't hit Julie too."

"Oh, don't worry about Julie. I took care of her." Or, rather, she took care of herself.

"Wait, you did? You have to tell us what happened." Jade leaned forward.

"I figured out that by blowing apart the tower, I could break the curse. By the time Julie showed up, the tower was about to crumble. She didn't realize that by killing Lady Naraka, she also destroyed the stairs. I watched her fall as I was escaping." I could still see the look of terror on her face.

"Whoa. That's crazy. Do you know what Lady Naraka wanted?" Jade asked.

"Yes, she wanted my magic." I leaned back in my bed. "Can I see my dad now?"

"Of course. We'll be back later." Jade hopped up, and Liz followed her out.

Katy stood and gave me a quick hug. "I'm glad you're back. Call us as soon as you're out of the hospital so we can hang out." She waved and left, passing a nurse who came to check on us.

I turned toward Mom. "Why were they in here instead of Dad?"

She laughed. "They were pretty insistent, and the nurses told them they could come in as long as they didn't wake you up."

"Thanks. I'm just glad Luke isn't here. I imagine I look pretty awful." I had bandages on my face and arms, and my whole body felt like one giant bruise. I reached for the mug of water on the table near me and took a large drink.

"You did things with magic I've never seen before, sweetie. You'll be exhausted for a while." She coughed again.

"Are you okay?" I asked.

"I'm doing much better now. Sitting in that dungeon with not much to eat for years really did me in. I'll be fine in a while."

"But I don't get it. You died. I went to the funeral." But then I remembered there had been no body. Tears welled up.

"Lady Naraka chained me up and threw my gown and locks of my hair out on the ground, covered in blood. She loved to tell me the story. She watched as your dad found everything and sobbed helplessly over what he thought was left of me. She laughed as hunters went searching through the forests." Mom had a coughing fit, and the nurse stepped in to offer water.

Dad came in the room, pulled up a chair between the two of us, and took Mom's hand. He looked happier than I'd ever seen him. He winked at me and turned back to Mom, silent as she continued the story.

"Every year, she would send people out to look for you, wanting to know if your magic had manifested itself yet. When you used your magic for the first time, she was thrilled, but she had to wait until you were old enough to be useful to her."

I'd been watched for that long? I shivered. No wonder the woman creeped me out. "And Dad didn't know about any of this?"

Mom picked at her blanket. Dad smiled at her and then turned to me. "I knew we were targeted, but I didn't know why. I figured it was just someone after my . . ." He stopped. "That's why we were in hiding. When your mother disappeared, I brought you here. All the business trips I've gone on over the years, I've really been going back to run things."

"What things? I don't get it." I watched Dad fidget and glance over at Mom. But then a memory from one of my dreams came back, and I grabbed on to it. "What does my grandma look like?"

"Which grandma?" Mom asked, surprised.

"In my dream the other day, I was able to make a room into a palace. I saw Dad talking to someone and saying we were going into hiding. The woman had long, dark hair that was starting to gray."

A tear went down Mom's cheek. "You saw my mom?"

I shrugged. "I guess. But that was at a castle. It didn't make any sense."

Dad cleared his throat. "Sweetheart, there's a reason I call you princess."

I laughed, but then stopped when I saw their expressions. "You have to be kidding me. You're trying to tell me I'm a . . . a princess? Give me a break." When they didn't smile, my laughter died off. "You're serious?" I started putting things together. Dad and Grandma. What Dad had said about running things.

Dad sighed and leaned forward, rubbing his neck. "I am the king of a small country near Switzerland. People don't know it exists because we're tucked away. We're more like rulers of a magical world."

If I'd thought my brain was going to explode before, it wasn't even close to this. "So you think Julie married you for your crown?" I glanced over at Mom. She looked away and wiped a tear.

"Possibly. What she didn't realize is that she would never have taken the throne. Neither would any of her children. There's an imprint in the magic of the king or queen that produces the next heir."

The word "imprint" sent a shock through me. All those times she tried to get me to pay her what she wanted, it had been a hoax. She didn't want gems or dresses or anything like them. "That's what she wanted," I exclaimed. "Lady Naraka told Nick she needed my imprint. She was trying to become queen."

Dad stood and paced. "That makes sense. And it would explain why Julie was insistent on staying around. She needed to keep an eye on you."

"I told you she was controlling you. And she tried to do it to me a few days before my party."

Dad nodded. "I understand that now. And I'm sorry for not listening."

Mom began weeping. "I made such a mess of your life. I'm so sorry."

I climbed out of bed and shuffled over to hers, ignoring the protests of the nurses. Mom scooted over so I could be next to her. "Mom, you did all this for me. Don't ever think you need to apologize."

She hugged me close. "I love you."

"I love you too, Mom." I looked over as one of the nurses cleared her throat. "Oh, sorry." She helped me out of Mom's bed and back into mine. She checked my blood pressure and then left the room. "So, Dad, will we go back to your—our—kingdom?"

Dad leaned forward in his chair. "That's up to you. I need to go back because it's been a while since I've visited, but you are free to finish school here."

I didn't want to leave just when things were starting to look up, but a castle? A real-live castle? And I was the princess. "I'd like to visit, at least. It's strange that I don't remember living there."

"Don't you? You'll have to think very carefully. You would run through the halls as fast as your legs could carry you, and the visiting dignitaries thought you were the cutest little girl alive."

"I don't remember." But what I did remember was the feeling of home when I'd made the room at camp.

My mind drifted between my friends, and it stopped on Luke. "So, wait. Who are Phil and Luke and everyone else? Are they just your coworkers here?"

Dad laughed. "No, they're all my best people from back home. Luke is the heir to the throne in another part of Europe. I brought him here to watch out for you while I was gone. And I admit that there may have been a little matchmaking involved."

Mom slapped his hand playfully. "Alex! You shouldn't be matchmaking. You remember how badly it almost turned out for you."

"Yeah, that was bad. Thankfully, you stepped in at just the right moment." He kissed her hand and laughed at my confused expression. "Let's just say that your grandmother tried to set me up with a rather . . . interesting princess from another kingdom. When she was caught stealing forks from the kitchen, Mom sent her away. Soon after, your mother came along and we hit it off."

"We'll talk about your matchmaking attempt for me later. But for now, I'm tired and I want my own bed. When do we get to go home?" I pulled up my blankets and settled in.

"We're just waiting for your mom. None of your injuries are serious, so you can leave when you're ready."

I was exhausted, and leaving Mom wasn't something I was ready to do yet. "I'll just stay here."

"All right, sweetie."

I closed my eyes to rest, but something still bothered me. "One more thing and then I'll drop it. Do we know what happened to Nick?"

Dad shrugged. "No one knows. The prison where your mom was kept wasn't fully part of the stairs. It's possible he escaped."

"I hope so. He was starting to grow on me. As irritating as he was."

A nurse came in with some painkillers and watched me take them. Once I had swallowed them, she insisted I go back to sleep. I was totally okay with those orders. I had years of sleep to catch up on.

Chapter Twenty-Two

"Come on, Mom. I can't wait to show you around the house." I ran to the front door and stopped just before turning the knob. I hadn't been home since my birthday. Mom had needed another week to recuperate, but she was already filling out from the food the hospital had given her.

"I'm coming, sweetie." She stopped to stare up at the home Dad and I had called our own for the last several years. "Wow, it's a shame we can't just stay here. It's beautiful."

"Wait until you see the backyard. I kept it just how you'd like it. I couldn't bear to have it any other way." He put his arm around Mom and led her into the house.

"Whoa." I walked inside to find that everything had been changed since we left. Any evidence of Julie, Sarah, and Kaylee had disappeared, and everything was spotless.

Dad caught my expression. "I asked Phil to take care of the house while we were gone. I wanted it ready to sell."

"They did a wonderful job with it." Mom wandered through the house before going into the kitchen, where she pulled out pots and pans.

Dad went over and kissed the top of her head. "What are you doing?"

"Cooking. I can't begin to tell you how much I've missed it. After the nasty stuff I've eaten for the last several years, I'm ready for a gourmet meal."

I sat at the bar. "I'm ready to watch you instead of me having to cook everything myself." I couldn't stop staring at her. I'd missed her for so long—it was strange to have her back. Her hair had many gray streaks through it and her eyes had a haunted look to them. I couldn't imagine what she went through for so many years.

She smiled when she noticed me staring. "I'm fine, sweetie."

I blushed. "It's not that. I'm just so happy you're back."

Dad put his arm around me. "You're not the only one, sweetheart. And I'm anxious to return to our country as a family so I don't have to leave all the time."

"I can live with that." I lit up suddenly. "Wait—does this mean I don't have to worry about my senior year?"

Mom chuckled. "Nice try. You'll have a tutor at the

castle. You have a lot of lessons to catch up on about ruling a kingdom."

"Sweet. That sounds so much better than algebra." I could just imagine the look on Mr. Stanger's face when he found out I wouldn't be coming back for his English class next year. But then, he'd wanted good things for me, right? "So who gets to tutor me? Mom?"

Dad cleared his throat. "Actually, you've met her— your great-grandmother. She appeared in your dreams a few times." When he saw my blank stare, he continued. "And at the Renaissance fair. I'm sorry I didn't tell you before, but it was part of the whole 'secret past' thing. Plus, I wasn't sure it was her until I had the chance to visit with her while you and Mom were in the hospital."

I didn't speak for a minute. The fortune-teller? I'd seen my great-grandma and I didn't even know? I didn't know whether to be thrilled or angry. "What—how—so, wait. She could go inside my dreams? I thought that didn't happen anymore."

"She won't tell me how she did it. You know, I hadn't even seen her for several years, and I actually thought she'd died." He shook his head. "What a surprise—and she's thrilled to be able to teach you."

The doorbell rang, and I hopped up to answer it. Luke stood on the doorstep, hands behind his back. His eyes lit up when he saw me.

"Hey, Sydney. Can we talk?"

My heart pounded, remembering the last time I'd seen him. I was afraid I'd lost him—and everything else—that night. "Of course." I went outside and shut the door. "How'd you know we were home?"

He smiled. "I have my ways. I hear you beat Julie and Lady Naraka at the same time. That takes some skill."

I shrugged. "Julie kind of did it to herself. But you should have seen the magic I was able to do." I grinned. "It was so cool destroying that tower."

Luke laughed. "I'm sure it was. You have some pretty intense magic." He paused. "But that's not why I came here."

"So, why *are* you here then?" I stepped forward.

His face turned red. "I, uh, I have something to ask."

"What's that?" I could barely breathe, wondering what it was. By the tenderness on his face, I had a feeling it was something good.

He pulled out the glass slipper I'd lost at the ball. "I found this right after you were ripped from my arms. I looked everywhere for the owner, but no one claimed it. I was kind of hoping you'd know where to find her."

"I'm pretty sure I could help you with that." My heart pounded even harder with excitement.

"May I?" He gestured toward the bench on the porch, his eyes dancing. All my questions about whether he liked me flew out the window. I'd thought I'd had a crush on him before, but now I knew I was totally and completely in love with him.

I sat and held my foot out for him. Tingles rushed through me as he gently pulled off my sneaker and then my sock and slid the glass slipper onto my foot. I smiled down at him. "Perfect fit."

"Well, what do you know?" He smiled up at me. "I found my princess."

The End

Also by Jaclyn Weist

The Luck Series

Stolen Luck

Twist of Luck

Best of Luck

More Than Just Luck

No Such Luck

Just My Luck

Lost in a Fairy Tale

Timeless

Fearless

Endless

Celtic Fairy Tale Romance

Leana

Keela

Gates of Atlantis (Middle Grade)

Magicians of the Deep

About the Author

Jaclyn is an Idaho farm girl who grew up loving to read. She developed a love for writing at a young age and published her first book in 2013. She met her husband, Steve, at BYU, and they have six happy, crazy children who encourage her to keep writing. After owning a bookstore and running away to have adventures in Australia, they settled back down in their home in Utah. Jaclyn now spends her days herding her kids to various activities and trying to remember what she was supposed to do next. Her books include Endless; Timeless; Fearless; Magicians of the Deep; Leana; Keela; and the Luck series, which helped feed her obsession with all things Irish.